BORN DIFFERENT

BORN DIFFERENT

A MONSTER EVOLUTION LITRPG

V. Nator

Podium

For my family,
who push me to be the best I can be by supporting my many silly interests.

Published in 2024 by Podium Publishing
www.podiumaudio.com

Podium

BORN DIFFERENT

CHAPTER ONE

Born into Darkness

Every few generations, a child comes into the world who is greater than their peers, being unparalleled in mind, body, or strength of their soul. But who is to say that this phenomenon does not also occur in monsters, those base creatures found beneath the Earth, or in the harsh and untamed wilderness? Perhaps in the form of a commanding matriarch amongst dire wolves, a terrible titan of the already massive frost ogres, or an uncatchable butcher bird? All are unparalleled threats that have claimed the lives of countless adventurers brought to greater heights. However, they are not the worst one can encounter.

The Noble Races of the surface gained their place above all others not through levels or magic, but through their minds. Our cunning intellect has raised us up to the apex of all species. If a monster was to be born in possession of our greatest blessing, there may very well be a new race to join our ranks.

—Estran Leabrar, discredited scholar of the Shostran Royal Palace

Darkness. It was everywhere, all-consuming nothingness. That was all that was. Even the mind that conceived of these notions did not exist. And then . . .

They did.

Limbs moved, kicked, pushed.

They felt.

They felt a barrier curving around them that resisted their kicks. They pushed at it as hard as they could.

They heard.

They heard the barrier crack and fall away, letting soft rays of blue light filter through the jagged opening.

They saw.

Within a few minutes, they were entirely free of the barrier, which lay around them in a pile of thin white shards.

They in this case was a single being, one elevated beyond a mere *it* by mind and sense of self.

And they were not alone.

Hundreds of limbs scurried around, covered in tiny hairs that rubbed across each other. Legs were scrambling around something . . . something delicious.

A powerful instinct drove the being towards sustenance. The being jumped and juked, ducked and wove through their brethren until they reached the carcass of a similar, though much larger, creature. The being opened their mandibles and took a bite, the knowledge of how to do it already inscribed in their brain.

Eventually, the body was consumed, and the many tiny spiders sat there, digesting their meal. They did not know what else to do, at least for the moment.

"*URRROAAAAHHHHH!*" came a baleful roar.

The spiders suddenly knew what to do and began to scurry. The arachnids scuttled past the white bars of a cage much too large to contain them and ran as far as their legs could carry them.

That one particular spider, on the other hand, opened their eyes and looked. Darkness loomed, broken up by the soft blue glow of tall bioluminescent mushrooms. The fungal stalks towered above the spider, each capable of turning the arachnid into paste if they were to ever fall over—not that any of them looked ready to with their sturdy trunks. Beyond the lights, paws and jaws waited. Teeth snatched up the other spiders, giving them no chance to scream or cry out. Not that the spiders could scream anyway.

Many were eaten, but plenty still survived and scurried toward some cover: beneath a boulder, inside a crack in the ground, or up the walls and into the shadows. This one particular spider simply stayed where they were, along with several others. Perfectly still. Watching.

Getting frustrated at the quick meals running off, the gloom-bound predators turned their hungry eyes to the spiders that remained. They licked their lips and leapt.

Thunk.

The white bars stopped the creatures in their tracks; the tightly formed pillars proved too strong to allow even the nimblest of their paws to pass through. Not that they were very nimble to begin with. Their reaching limbs were nothing more than clubs that were still too weak to break through the dusty white.

Just as well. An even more powerful instinct told that one particular spider to seek shelter before realizing they were already in it. The others alongside them were simply too busy chewing on the leftover chitin of their meal to move.

If this newborn spider could scoff or roll their eyes, they already would have. Instead, they simply processed the novel feelings of frustration and disappointment.

But as they looked at the inedible pieces of chitin, they felt something new. The material looked the same as that of the spiders chewing on it; that made it . . . a parent. A bigger version of them, which had created this brood. And sacrificed its body to provide nourishment.

This one spider in particular felt a wave of relief that their parent was smart enough to lay its eggs in such a safe location—in this strangely shaped, yet effective barrier.

They looked around and saw pillars curved to form an oval-shaped shell that connected to a single, long fallen pillar, which extended to an eerie-looking growth at the very top. It looked similar to one of the predators that was staring them down; eyes and a tongue would fit into the holes in that growth.

The spider performed a mental shrug. Whatever the nature of this structure was, it was safe inside. It was home.

System Active

Juvenile Dungeon Spider (Level 1)	
Soul Link	Rockfort Hamlet Dungeon Core [????????]
Classes	N/A

Attributes	
Health	1/1
Body	1
Intellect	1
Soul	. . .

CHAPTER TWO

A Newborn Spider's Search for Food

Modern day adventurers are too picky. With cheap and plentiful survival rations, or any naturalist spellcaster worth their silver who can conjure up food, keeping an entire team's stomachs filled is a trivial task. When no such options exist, one is forced to live off the land.

Nomadic tribes and survivors from long ago were masters of such arts; they turned merely surviving off of the bounty of the seas or soil into thriving. They perfected the artform of cooking with what's on hand, and there is plenty to learn from them.

So follow me on a journey to see how you can take a few cave roots and some wild boar fat and turn them into a feast fit for a lord!

—Excerpt from *Wilderness Thriving* by Wes Stout, [Culinary Survivalist], first of his Class

The spider did not like waiting.

It was safe within their home, but there was a feeling of restlessness—a sense that they needed to be doing something, anything; and *nothing* wasn't something.

Nothing felt terrible. It wasn't instinct either; the restlessness occupied their consciousness—not that they could really describe what that was, but they knew how they felt. They felt bored.

And as if granted by the divine, the arachnid's prayer was answered. They now felt hungry.

The spider looked back to where the remains of their gracious parent were and saw chunks of its chitin scattered around their home. None of it was edible, but that didn't stop their siblings from trying. Those siblings had since left the safety of home to venture out for more food.

The spider looked around and felt pressure from their legs as they raised their abdomen in a frustrated acceptance. Rather than immediately rush out like their other, mostly eaten, brethren, the thoughtful arachnid took another few moments to look around.

Many hours had passed, and the large predators had since left for elsewhere. Perhaps the large creatures had their own homes, their own safe havens? Either way, the predators were not here, and the way to food was safe.

The spider slowly stepped out from between the white pillars that marked their home, legs primed to jump back to safety at the smallest sign of trouble. They waited for several seconds, attentive and ready to flee. However, there was no need.

If they could have sighed, they would have. Instead, a small pop of relief and happiness flashed in their mind and faded away as they remembered the danger that still surrounded them.

*Right…*The arachnid took another step, then another until they were several feet away from the safety of their home. If they were to be ambushed by one of the predators now, their speed would not allow them to get away in time. A wave of hunger spiked through the spider's stomach; they didn't have a choice.

When the predators first attacked, the spider had seen that they only went for those in the open, the ones that walked past them. Those that had made it into the shadows or up the walls had stayed safe, but the nearest walls were well past where our lone spider was comfortable going. So, to the shadows it went.

The arachnid darted between errant rocks and stalagmites, careful to avoid the glow of the towering mushrooms. Though the bright fungus would have made it easier to find morsels, they didn't want to risk bringing attention to themself. After all, it didn't take a genius to figure out that light was the opposite of dark. The spider was born just yesterday, and even *they* knew so.

But even with the help of the light, it would still not be easy to find a meal—mostly because the spider didn't know what a meal looked like, exactly. Food was supposed to be covered in chitin and filled with a rotting mush, right? No, there had to be something better out there.

Though the actual best marker would, of course, have been taste, the arachnid didn't exactly know *what* to try and taste. Instinct said nothing about the world in this instance.

The lone spider attempted to bite into a rock, but the feelings were unpleasant. Their tiny fangs hurt, and the taste . . . They couldn't describe it. But it wasn't good. Definitely not good.

They continued on, looking for something, anything that they could eat. And they found it.

Wriggling on the ground was a miniscule creature. It had no chitin, no legs, and was pink. Such a creature could not possibly exist. How had it not been eaten yet?

The arachnid approached the strange being and observed. It moved forward little by little, seemingly without any particular destination in mind. Did it even have a mind?

They didn't really care, because, as if flipped by a switch, instinct kicked in, and the spider bit into the pink creature. It writhed in their grip but only when they lifted it into the air. It did not feel. The spider bit it again until it stopped moving and felt a spark of joy at their first earned meal.

Experience +1 | Next Level: 1/5

There was that feeling again, but it was more than merely a feeling. What even was that? Words and numbers held no meaning for spiders. But alongside the symbols they received the raw meaning and the feeling behind the numbers. "Promised improvement" was the best way to describe the sensation: a potential yet to be realized. It seemed to be saying that something would happen when something else filled up. The "thing" had filled up a bit when they killed the pink creature, and judging by the full sensation, they would have to kill four more to fill it completely. But what exactly would happen? Whatever it was, they began to feel giddy.

The arachnid quickly tossed those thoughts aside, as what they were *really* looking forward to was the meal in front of them. The spider opened their mandibles to take their first bite.

They clamped their jaws shut around . . . nothing.

A force impacted our spider, causing them to jump, and the ground rumbled around them.

After landing back down, their eyes quickly opened and scanned their surroundings. The spider's legs worked overtime, pushing in all directions to avoid any claws or jaws—but none of those came. Instead, they saw another spider. This one had the same color, chitin, and number of legs. But it was bigger. And holding the earthworm within its mandibles.

Our spider stared in horror as their meal was eaten by one of their brethren. Shamelessly, it pulled the pink creature into its mouth and stomach while it hopped around in mirth. Here was a spider that had discovered the wonderful art of delegation as well as the use of force in achieving one's desires. Our spider was very jealous.

But this newcomer was kind enough to teach the lone spider these same lessons with another shove. The message was clear: "Bring me food because I'm bigger than you." The smaller spider had no choice but to accept, because as they continued to look for food, the larger spider followed closely behind them, making sure it was not cheated of its prize.

And hunting was not the only work the smaller arachnid had to do.

The larger spider's eyes were so closely locked on them that it wasn't even watching its surroundings. Our spider thought of leading it to a predator, but they remembered the greed of *those* creatures and how eating one spider wouldn't be enough for any of them.

The two eventually came across another piece of prey: a small, chitin-covered insect that walked along the ground. The smaller spider looked back at their larger sibling; it simply stared back with impatience, as if asking what they were waiting for. Our spider felt true frustration for the first time and clicked their mandibles once, making a low ringing sound. They bit at the insect, killing it in one strike.

Experience +1 | Next Level: 2/5

Before the spider could do anything else, they were lifted into the air and forced to let go of their quarry. They were then tossed to the side as their larger sibling walked over to the insect's corpse and ate it.

The spider clicked their mandibles again. What even was the point of this idiot following them around and keeping such a close eye if hunting its own meals would have taken just as much effort? From such an early age, the previously lone spider understood the concept of micromanaging and how utterly terrible it was.

CHAPTER THREE

Finding a Competitive Edge

"Survival of the fittest" was a phrase coined by a legendary researcher on monster evolution in reference to monster hierarchies, which was then grossly misinterpreted by unqualified life scholars and adventurers everywhere to mean something completely unrelated.

The phrase refers to how it is the most capable of monsters that evolve into their stronger forms. A tribe of goblins might have a physically strongest member, but it is the one that gains the most Experience that actually transforms into a hobgoblin. Fitness, in this case, refers to how capable a monster is of gaining Experience and not how big its muscles are.

Yet some of you aren't even smart enough to understand optimal Experience gain, even with a world-class teacher, whereas many monsters do it by instinct! Real-world experience could work for you, but at the same time, I think I know what kind of strategy you would all settle on. Repetition in combat leads to plateaus in both wisdom and System

Experience; thus, there is only so much you all will gain from hitting the same tiny creature a hundred times!

**—Excerpt from a lecture by retired adventurer
Arturius Finnegan to a group of novices**

Another bug.

Another kill.

Another theft.

This particular spider didn't like these events. But one thing did make up for it.

> Experience +1 | Next Level: 3/5

The sensation brought forth another strange new emotion: hope. A feeling that said there would be happiness to come. Not now, which was quite frustrating; but the idea of happiness in the future brought some bit of happiness to the present.

Too bad happiness wasn't enough to fill a stomach. Our particular spider let out another lone *click*.

Huh. The click described the feelings behind the sound quite well. *Click*. That was who this particular spider was: Click.

Click scurried along the ground, careful to keep an eye out for predators and to stick to the shadows as their sibling lumbered just behind them like some great big oaf. When they found a meal in a small insect or worm, their bigger brother was the one to eat it, not even leaving a single limb or drop of blood for their smaller sibling.

When Click found meal number four, they decided to do something different. They turned away from the worm and sat down.

Their older brother looked at the two in silent confusion for a few seconds, trying to contemplate what it should do. It had never experienced such a dilemma, having been born just yesterday. So, it did the only thing it knew how.

Click felt a shove and landed on their back. It took a moment before they could right themself, and Click found their brother staring right at them. The brother made a single click with its mandibles.

Click clicked back. Clicking was *their* thing!

Their brother clicked and shoved again.

A new series of emotions erupted within Click's mind: indignation at being treated this way, defiance at what was nothing more than a pathetic enemy, and sheer rage at their brother's utter stupidity. The meal was *right there*! What did it need Click for when it could just *kill and eat it right now*!

The world once again flew around our spider in a terrible whirl before they hit the ground.

And Click felt one more emotion as they ended another small life and forwent their rightful meal: exasperation.

Experience +1	Next Level: 4/5

Click didn't even wait for their brother to finish eating before running off in search of meal number five. The larger spider gave chase with the fruits of Click's labor still sticking out of its mouth, making it look ridiculous as it raced after its sibling.

Click didn't care, and soon found their next target: another insect. This one was different from the others. Despite its miniscule stature, it was aware enough to sense the oncoming spider and dig its way underneath a rock.

Click jumped down the hole to follow and, after a moment, realized something felt off. They were alone. A click echoed from the hole's entrance while an annoyed-looking spider gazed in. It couldn't fit.

Click lifted their mandibles in a facsimile of a smile, an action that had nothing to do with the human motion but meant the same. If they had had a middle finger, they would've lifted it too.

The solitude was nice, especially in the safety of the enclosed space and darkness. But they were there for a reason: to get themself a meal.

The insect was easy to find. It likely wasn't as aware as Click thought it was, since it didn't try to run as the spider approached. Perhaps it was just instinct that led it down into this hole.

It was also instinct that led Click to drive their mandibles into the creature and drain it of its innards, finally granting them their first meal.

Experience +1 | Next Level: 5/5

Level up!

Level requirement achieved for evolution

Only one choice available. Automatically selecting: Juvenile Dungeon Spider

CHAPTER FOUR

Just Deserts

There has always been a divide between soldiers and adventurers in how they handle combat. War, as messy as it is, can be very predictable. An army consists of a definite number of troops with specific strengths and abilities. Given that there are no ambushes or reinforcements, it is possible to calculate a suitable force that will counter and defeat a known army with minimal casualties.

But adventurers don't fight people; they fight monsters. And monsters can evolve.

An infamous example of this unpredictability comes from a cautionary tale, often recounted to young adventurers, of a novice group sent to slay a small lounge of Armorscale Lizards. These lizards had been driven from their home into human-inhabited lands due to forest fires. The adventurers expected an easy fight, for their party was properly outfitted and leveled enough to be more than a match for these displaced creatures.

However, during the fight, one of the lizards evolved—caused, perhaps, by an opportunity taken to eat a stray insect or something else—after an unseen kill granted just enough Experience to trigger a level up and subsequent transformation.

With strife comes strength, and this Armorscale Lizard had been through plenty after surviving the forest fires and the fights brought about by the resulting move. That strength evolved the lizard into the rare Armorscale Salamander, which was a tier above the adventurers.

It was a miracle that there even was a survivor, but their story keeps others from meeting the same fate. So, be happy that enemy soldiers won't suddenly transform into fire-breathing behemoths and burn you all alive. The worst they can do is stab you.

—Excerpt from a guest lecture at the Shostran Royal Military Academy by Commander Valencia Yoltide, specialist in adventurer relations

Beginning evolution . . .

A strange and forceful feeling enveloped Click, something that took over their body. Not to say they'd lost control as they could still move their limbs. But *that* was the issue: those weren't their limbs. At least, not as they had been a moment ago. And it wasn't just their limbs. Their entire body began to change. The thorax, abdomen, head, all eight legs, everything! Something was happening inside of them.

When the sensation faded, Click was left . . . different. Knowledge of what was different came to them.

Juvenile Dungeon Spider (Level 2)	
Name	Click
Soul Link	Rockfort Hamlet Dungeon Core [????????]
Classes	N/A

Attributes	
Health	3/3
Body	2
Intellect	151
Soul	3

Skill unlocked: Venom Gland
Skill unlocked: Silk Spinning

Level 1: Venom Gland
Secrete a toxic substance from the mandibles that can harm lesser creatures.

Level 1: Silk Spinning
Secrete a sticky string that can ensnare weaker creatures.

Click felt . . . good. It was more than good, in fact; the sensation was utterly euphoric, and there was even more to it!

As they raised their mandibles once again, the sound of digging began to echo out from the entrance. The hole began to expand, and soon Click's larger sibling made its way inside. It saw the drained insect carcass and stared at Click incomprehensibly. Had they . . . *dared* to eat its meal?!

It walked over to Click and shoved them. Click didn't budge.

It shoved them again. Once again, nothing.

Click shoved back, and the spider went flying. When it finally hit the ground with a thud, it realized what had happened.

Click had grown up.

Click placed a leg on their sibling's abdomen and pushed it down before it had a chance to run. It writhed on the ground, and Click felt nothing but pity; they didn't even apply any actual force. When the movement stopped, Click removed their leg and lifted up their sibling, carrying it out of the hole. Once in the open, Click pointed the other spider towards a wide open area filled with several insects.

It got the message. It was *its* turn to go hunting for someone else.

The spider scurried into the open area and leapt on a bug while Click stood behind the rock. As their sibling captured its prey and considered the unforgivable sin of simply eating it, a fuzzy paw large enough to grab a dozen spiders came flying down and pinned it to the ground. The greedy sibling was soon dead and tossed inside of the predator's mouth.

There was a reason Click didn't hunt out there, despite it being filled to the brim with potential food. Besides, they didn't want their brethren to grow like they just had; it wouldn't be good to have the tables turned back so soon.

CHAPTER FIVE

New Skills, New Prey, New Way of Life

The System is subject to much scrutiny, but very few answers have been found.

The clergy would call it a gift of the divine, yet it is also given to the very monsters that hunt the Noble Races. The numerical representations of its values are the subject of close study by mathematicians, who can only scratch the surface of their meanings; and yet, unintelligent beasts utilize these to maximum efficiency.

Do those very numbers reflect our own natural abilities, or simply what the System adds onto it? Where does the System end and biology begin, if it ends at all?

Understanding all of this has sadly been written off as a fool's errand, with many choosing to simply accept it. Those very people may cite the definite crassness of looking a gift horse in the mouth, but learning how to ride that very horse? That is a compliment to whomever provided this gift.

—Speech by Horatio Sutherland, System scholar of the Shostran Royal Academy, one year before his early retirement

Click's hunt was semi-successful. Sure, their belly wasn't exactly filled after eating only one tiny insect, but something had happened after their fifth kill. They had grown bigger and stronger. They had evolved.

And with that increased size came an increased appetite.

Click's stomach wasn't designed to growl, but their nerves were hooked up well enough to tell them that they were hungry. They didn't have any accompanying mannerisms—no grabbing their abdomen and bending over or giving off pitiful glances to their parent to eke out a snack from the pantry. Besides, the arachnid's progenitor had already done everything to feed Click. They were quite grateful for that.

The spider strutted past their home in search of another meal, the protective white pillars feeling slightly smaller as they passed by. Only a small handful of other spiders were inside. They looked tired, as if they'd just barely managed to escape some predator or other and were taking respite within the safety of their home.

The other spiders must have been smart enough to avoid predators entirely and were most likely still hunting. Five kills wouldn't take long for them to achieve, especially against those unaware earthworms, so the others had most likely evolved as well and were looking for something to fill *their* stomachs.

Click ventured back into the deeper parts of the cave.

It didn't take them long to find another meal and capture it, thanks to their much longer legs. But the worm they found looked . . . smaller. No, it was the same size. Click was just bigger. The worm went limp in the spider's fangs as a faint blue liquid flowed into its body.

> Skill level up! Venom Gland (2)

Venom, that was what it was. Click understood the meaning behind the notification. They could do something new that they couldn't before, something *very* different. The worm went flying into their mouth and down without needing to chew. It didn't even begin to fill them up. Click *was* bigger.

Too big.

Or maybe the prey was too small?

Experience +1 | Next Level: 1/50

Click settled down next to a rock and began to survey the cave. The bugs they had been going for earlier were plentiful, but the time it would take to chase so many down was unappealing. But something quickly caught their attention: bigger bugs.

Click charged at one, jaws open wide and ready to bite.

The insect nimbly hopped away. Strong legs carried it several times higher than the spider's height and far away from danger.

The arachnid clicked their jaws together once, knowing that they weren't the only one to benefit from an increased size. They turned to another larger yet edible bug. This one's legs were much smaller, but most of its mass was located in its abdomen. It would be much too heavy to get away!

Click charged at it with even greater speed, but as their fangs were about to envelop the insect, its chitinous shell parted to reveal a pair of wings that quickly carried it away.

Click.

Another spider of similar size to Click jumped at the bug and made contact. Its fangs covered the insect and pulled it into its maw. By the time it landed, the flying creature was no more. Instead, eight legs thick with hydraulic fluid and supporting a sturdy torso stood tall.

Click couldn't help but feel self-conscious in the presence of such a physically capable specimen of their species. *That* was a new emotion.

The other spider gracefully scurried away, leaving Click with a sudden distaste. Their instincts pushed them to jump at every potential meal with venom-bearing fangs, but it was obvious that it wasn't working out for them. Maybe it was time to try something different?

Click headed back home, hoping for a safe place to think, and passed by several of their brethren along the way. They were suspended in mid-air, stock still. No, that wasn't right. Click focused their eyes and saw a thin filament holding them up. Webbing!

Click instinctively understood how to produce webbing and that it was difficult for non-spiders to escape it. However, Click felt the strong urge to use venom instead. It was a stupid urge if it wasn't going to get them anything to eat.

After the mental equivalent of a dark-alley mugging, the spider forced the dormant part of their instinct to cough up the knowledge behind optimal web placement and got to work. They ignored their headache and began to spin a sticky net between a chipped stalagmite and the ground.

Skill level up! Silk Spinning (2)
Skill level up! Silk Spinning (3)
Skill level up! Silk Spinning (4)

The end result was quite nice, if a little oblong. Click climbed to the top of it and settled in, eyes still vigilant for any predators. They waited in place for several seconds, followed by minutes, and then hours.

Okay, maybe not hours, but it was still ridiculous. The spider turned to look at their brethren and saw that they were having similar luck, but none of them were shuffling with the frantic energy Click was. The others were stock still, utterly serene and tranquil, as if waiting for prey to fall into their nets was all that they expected out of life.

What kind of life was that?

Click jumped down from the net and their head began to twitch as they looked for some prey. Click didn't think anything was wrong with them but began to feel like they and the other web-bound brethren were from completely different species. Click couldn't ignore that instinct. When they found a jumping bug some distance away, the arachnid felt the urge to chase after it. The spider took one step before clamping down on that very instinct and instead walked around it.

They'd made it a full semi-circle around before letting loose and chasing after the insect with their fangs bared. The bug inevitably jumped, but it never hit the ground. Another one of Click's jumping brethren tried to grab it but missed. Instead, the bug landed in Click's web.

The other spider stared at the stuck bug, as if trying to comprehend how the creature could be suspended in mid-air like that. That gave Click ample time to shove their sibling aside and reach their net, quickly sinking their fangs into the insect and draining it.

Experience +5 | Next Level: 6/50

Click actually began to feel a little satisfied. Just a little.
And dessert was nice too.

CHAPTER SIX

Understanding Idiots

As a mother, I must say that the state of education in the Shostran Kingdom is in need of refinement. That isn't to say that the wonderful schools in the capital are doing a bad job, mind you, but I mean education as a whole.

There are a lot of young men coming into town from out in the wilderness. I mean, they don't call it the wilderness, since they're technically from civilization, but it's still just a rural village! Where was I? Oh, right, these young men. They work alongside the men and women who grew up in the capital under your expert tutelage, but they have their own ways of doing things.

Huh? Is it more effective? That's not what I'm talking about. I'm saying they're different, and they're throwing off the established order of things! That's why I propose that all of the schools in the kingdom teach the same things. They have to follow the same format if we want everyone to learn the same so they can do the same job!

What do you mean, you can't control what other schools teach? What if those kids are taught by their parents or some volunteer schoolmarm? It's your duty to your kingdom to raise the next generation, and I don't want my dear son, Jadelyin, to be working alongside someone who doesn't know how things are supposed to be done! If you won't do it, I'll bring this to the king himself!

—Notes from a Parent–Teacher Association meeting at Saint Coteslia Elementary School

Why is nobody else doing this? Click thought to themself as they chased a small group of jumping bugs towards their web.

The sticky silk structure was built low, so the final push had to be very light lest the insects jump all the way over. Doing so wasn't too difficult; it only took Click two tries to realize this.

The spider took a deep breath and admired their handiwork. A dozen bugs sat in their web while those of their brethren were all just about empty. What did they expect, building so close to each other and just sitting there?

Well, no matter. Click flexed their mandibles in a smile and walked over to their meal. Before they could climb up and grab what was rightfully theirs, they were thrown by a powerful shove.

No, a shove wasn't what threw them; it was a tidal wave of spiders! As Click got back up, they saw that the other spiders were climbing all over Click's significantly fuller web. The arachnids' legs shuffled over each other in a writhing mass around the captured insects, which could do naught but squirm before being quickly wrapped up and devoured by hungry maws.

Experience +3 | Next Level: 9/50
Experience +3 | Next Level: 12/50
Experience +3 | Next Level: 15/50
. . .
Level up!

Juvenile Dungeon Spider (Level 3)	
Name	Click
Soul Link	Rockfort Hamlet Dungeon Core [????????]
Classes	N/A

Attributes	
Health (+1)	4/4
Body (+1)	3
Intellect (+1)	152
Soul (+1)	4

The notifications were the only thing keeping Click from going over and biting the first spider they could get their venomous mandibles on.

But as the viciously lazy thieves devoured Click's hard-earned feast, they noticed something . . . or rather, a lack of something. The webs that the freeloaders had constructed lay completely empty of both meals and their weavers. In other words: it was free real estate.

Click scurried on over to the closest abandoned web and gave it a good hard look. It was big, but its weave prioritized taking up space instead of making good use of it. That wouldn't do. It only took two or three extra strands of spider silk, and the web was widened and heightened to be able to catch airborne insects. Whoever had first woven the web had done all of the hard work; this was more akin to putting a bow on top. And that bow was much easier to place than it would have been when they first started.

Skill level up! Silk Spinning (5)

Click looked over to their old web and saw that their brethren had resorted to fighting each other for what was left. Click would've made a scoffing noise if they had had the appropriate vocal cords; instead, they resorted to making a single click with their mandibles.

Click quickly put aside the negative feelings, and after a quick run, their new web was filled with just as many bugs as the last one. They marveled at the results of their hard work and got ready to jump in with the captured bugs. But Click wasn't the only one admiring the work.

The spider turned their eyes to their old web to see their brethren watching intently as this new one filled up. The slightly bigger web held exactly the same number of morsels as the last one had, but the spiders simply stood watching.

Click's eyes and mandibles flashed a fierce warning—one that was entirely ignored, as all gazes were locked on the web. A lone insect idly flew through the air, and, in an attempt to mate with one of the others of its species, got caught up in the same trap.

Click knew what was about to happen. They felt it deep in their gut and hoped that they were wrong.

They were right.

It was the straw that broke the spider's back; a swarm of legs and hungry fangs jumped down and ran at the successful new web.

Click, the lone spider responsible for the captured food, opened their mandibles and let out the closest imitation of a scream they could muster—a primal expression of their unyielding rage and indignation. They jumped into the throng and began to bite.

The stampede didn't care much and granted one mercy by throwing Click off to the side rather than trampling them to death.

Click fell to their belly in defeat as they watched their hard work devoured right before their eyes. All of that time and effort spent and once again, with nothing to show for it.

Experience +3 | Next Level: 18/55
Experience +3 | Next Level: 21/55
Experience +3 | Next Level: 24/55
. . .
Level up!

Juvenile Dungeon Spider (Level 4)	
Name	Click
Soul Link	Rockfort Hamlet Dungeon Core [????????]
Classes	N/A

Attributes	
Health (+1)	5/5
Body (+1)	4
Intellect (+0)	152
Soul (+1)	5

Experience? But how? Click thought. All they had done was chase the insects into somebody else's web! They knew that chasing one of those bugs didn't count for anything after that one physically gifted spider had eaten the bug Click had been pursuing. And this particular web only had one or two strands that were actually *from* Click. The rest were woven by . . .

One of the spiders in the throng grew ever so slightly and used their new advantage to push one of their brethren off the web.

Maybe Experience was doled out to *anyone* who contributed to a web? But in that case . . .

Click quickly ran over to the other silken nets. These ones were woven very close to each other, so with only a few strings they could be turned into a single web. And that was just what Click did. And this time, the spider wasn't worried, for one very simple reason.

Click *knew* what would make their brethren attack. Click had felt the urge themself, after all. Right as that last insect had landed on the web, some kind of mental switch had been flipped that made Click want to run over and gorge themself on every single insect they could get their hands on. It wasn't based on the raw number of bugs, since both webs had the same amount, but the second web hadn't triggered the swarm's frenzy until that last bug had landed. The only difference between the webs was their size. It was the *density* of the bugs that triggered it.

Click didn't have a word to describe "density." They didn't have *any* words for that matter. But the concept of how closely stuff was squished together was easy enough to understand. And the spider knew exactly how squished-together things needed to be before their brethren would run over. Click would just have to underfill the web.

Skill level up! Silk Spinning (6)
Skill level up! Silk Spinning (7)
Skill level up! Silk Spinning (8)

A few more minutes passed, and the spider was ready to collapse. Their mega-web was filled to the brim with insects, but with plenty of space between them. The other spiders looked over but stayed on Click's old web, looking over with a mix of jealousy and hunger. Yet, they did not move. They waited.

They waited while Click slowly made their way up the mega-structure and took their first bite. The lone spider savored their meal and scuttled over to the next. And the next. Their energy was returning to them and with it, a feeling of glee.

Experience +5 | Next Level: 10/60
Experience +5 | Next Level: 15/60
Experience +5 | Next Level: 20/60

. . .

These webs used to be theirs, but it wasn't Click's fault they'd made such a terrible trade deal.

Level up!

Juvenile Dungeon Spider (Level 5)	
Name	Click
Soul Link	Rockfort Hamlet Dungeon Core [????????]
Classes	N/A

Attributes	
Health (+1)	6/6
Body (+1)	5
Intellect (+1)	153
Soul (+1)	6

CHAPTER SEVEN

Picking Your Future Career at Two Days Old!

Many species across the world are blessed with access to the System, but only the Noble Races have been granted the ability to utilize Classes. From generic and humble professions to specialized roles and careers, Classes encompass just about all paths one can walk in life. So much so that many consider this offered versatility to be what makes the Noble Races greater than the rest.

They are wrong.

Monsters may not have access to Classes, but they have an even greater tool: evolution. The ability to morph one's own body, to become a different creature entirely, is powerful. Even more so when the transformations can be chosen in a way that complements one's abilities.

A warrior with natural talent for carrying great weight may take up the mantle of [Titan Knight] to make the best use of it, thanks to the Class's benefit of heavy armor and massive weapons. They still must purchase their arms and armor, not to mention gain proficiency in them through

repeated practice. But a Demon Rhino with similar talents?
They merely become a [Death Titan Rhino].

—Estran Leabrar, discredited scholar
of the Shostran Royal Palace

Click couldn't eat another bite. After figuring out that it was insect density that had triggered their brethren to ditch their old webs for Click's, the spider had put together a mega-web and filled it with just enough bugs to keep under the limit. It might not sound like much, but the vast space the web took up meant that there was a veritable feast! More than Click could eat, in fact.

Which was all well and good, as Click didn't quite eat the bugs; they sucked their innards dry. The spider took another sip and was greeted by a flurry of notifications.

Experience +5 | Next Level: 60/60
Level up!

Juvenile Dungeon Spider (Level 6)	
Name	Click
Soul Link	Rockfort Hamlet Dungeon Core [????????]
Classes	N/A

Attributes	
Health (+1)	7/7
Body (+1)	6
Intellect (+0)	153
Soul (+1)	7

Level requirement achieved for evolution
Choices available: Juvenile Dungeon Web Spider, Juvenile Dungeon Hunter Spider, Juvenile Dungeon Ambush Trapper Spider, Juvenile

> Dungeon Spider Commander
> Please select an option

Huh? Click scuttled over to a safe corner of their web and considered the . . . not-quite words. They felt a powerful compulsion towards the second choice and some amount of pull towards the third, but the prospect of there being a choice at all made them think. Especially since that prospect somehow imparted the understanding that it would be *important.*

Click had already experienced evolution once, but that had only resulted in getting bigger. This . . . was something different. The first question they asked was what the differences between each of these choices were.

> System query received. Producing result . . .
> Listing result (1/4): Advanced Evolution Overview

Juvenile Dungeon Web Spider	
Evolution Prerequisites	
Species	Juvenile Dungeon Spider

Base Attributes	
Health	10
Body	5
Intellect	2
Soul	2

Venom Gland
Secrete a toxic substance from the mandibles that can harm lesser creatures.

Silk Spinning
Secrete a sticky string that can ensnare weaker creatures.

Web Sense
Feel vibrations through created webs, even when not on them.

Those were a lot of concepts and . . . numbers? Click had never properly paid attention to numbers before but could wrap their brain around the idea behind them. Something about how *many* of something there were, like how *many* bugs Click could eat at once. The answer to that was about two dozen, by the way.

The concepts associated with each number made sense. *Health* was how many hits they could take without dying. That was easy to understand. It was accompanied by a sensation of vitality that Click could feel grow every time they leveled up and gained points in the attribute; it was like they simply *knew* they could take a bigger hit and keep going. Not that the spider was ever going to test it out.

Body came with a sensation of expansion and told how well Click could move around and how hard they could bite. Click had a body, and the attribute described its strength. While the spider's previous evolution had increased their body's size, that wasn't as big an indicator of the attribute as their hydraulic muscles, which felt changed on a more fundamental level; they were stronger and more efficient. Click didn't fully understand how they worked on the inside and hadn't given it any thought over the two days they'd been alive, but the sensation still gave them an idea that whatever was there was now better.

After that was *Intellect*, which came with an improved feeling of mental alacrity. Their most recent increase to the Intellect attribute felt more akin to a drop in an already vast ocean, but Click could still make out the difference in how it affected their own thinking. Thoughts were processed just a bit faster, the numbers attached to the attributes held just that much more meaning, and the world began to make a little more sense. It really wasn't much, but it was still noticeable.

And finally, there was *Soul*, or . . . some kind of alternate form of strength? While the other attributes were simple to understand because they correlated to the easily comprehensible parts of Click, Soul was linked to something beyond that. It was the strangest of them all, and

Click had no way to properly gauge what it actually did, let alone how much better they had become at whatever it was used for. The only way to really describe it was that Click felt a stronger sense of self. They were Click. Click was them.

Well, of course I'm me! And I like being me. Who else would I be? I'm great!

The spider paused for a moment as they went back to thinking.

So, what were those values, anyway? Click was starting to understand the idea behind these numbers and how different values, well . . . differed.

System query received. Producing result . . .
Listing result (1/3): In-Depth Evolution Attributes

Juvenile Dungeon Web Spider

Evolution Prerequisites

Species	Juvenile Dungeon Spider

Base	**Per level**	**Attribute**
10	1	Health
5	1	Body
2	1	Intellect
2	1	Soul

Venom Gland
Secrete a toxic substance from the mandibles that can harm lesser creatures.

Silk Spinning
Secrete a sticky string that can ensnare weaker creatures.

Web Sense
Feel vibrations through created webs, even when not on them.

Listing result (2/3): In-Depth Evolution Attributes

Juvenile Dungeon Spider		
Base	**Per level**	**Attribute**
2	2	Health
1	1	Body
0	0.5	Intellect
2	1	Soul

Listing result (3/3): Current Bonuses
Value | Bonus
+150 | Once in a Generation (Intellect)

It made a bit more sense to Click now. The value for an attribute was base + (per level x level count) + bonus, or times the bonus if it was percentage based. That meant something like Intellect for Click was 0 + (0.5 x 5) + 150, which was 152.5, which probably got rounded down to 152. Having only part of a number for a stat felt weird to Click, so it made sense that it would be a whole number.

The only bonus Click had was Intellect, and it was even gold in color! The spider lamented not having anything else and considered trading the massive +150 for something more useful, but the spider felt that it was because of the bonus that they could even think such things at all. Click shook their head and decided to be thankful for their blessings instead.

But it would be nice to show the per level information without asking.

Query received: change to display

Click spread their mandibles in a smile. Being listened to for once felt nice, and the spider motioned for the System to continue its previous information.

Listing result (2/4): Advanced Evolution Overview

Juvenile Dungeon Hunter Spider	
Evolution Prerequisites	
Species	Juvenile Dungeon Spider

Base	Per level	Attribute
10	2	Health
7	2	Body
1	0.5	Intellect
2	1	Soul

Venom Gland
Secrete a toxic substance from the mandibles that can harm lesser creatures.

Silk Spinning
Secrete a sticky string that can ensnare weaker creatures.

Prey Detection
Instinctually sense the location of prey and its movements.

Why were my instincts telling me to get this? Click furiously clicked their mandibles together at the idea of them almost picking such a terrible evolution over the others. The spider didn't need the extra points in Body or the [Prey Detection] Skill; they were doing *great* at getting food for themself! *This instinct of mine is completely useless! Pah. What's next?*

Listing result (3/4): Advanced Evolution Overview

Juvenile Dungeon Ambush Trapper Spider	
Evolution Prerequisites	
Species	Juvenile Dungeon Spider

Skill: Venom Gland	> Level 1
Skill: Silk Spinning	> Level 1

Base	Per level	Attribute
10	2	Health
7	2	Body
2	1	Intellect
2	1	Soul

Venom Gland
Secrete a toxic substance from the mandibles that can harm lesser creatures.

Silk Spinning
Secrete a sticky string that can ensnare weaker creatures.

Web Launch
Hold and throw your webbing.

Now *this* evolution was better in every way from the hunter spider! Why anyone would choose to take that route was beyond Click. Besides having the best of both worlds for Body *and* Intellect from both of the previous choices, the [Web Launch] Skill looked incredibly useful. Click could never catch anything on foot. But a thrown web would completely get rid of that disadvantage! But . . .

The spider stepped out of their little alcove and looked at their mega-web and the dozens of insects that covered it. Click felt the urge to laugh at the idea of actually needing the Skill.

So that just left one more choice. Click was relatively satisfied with the attribute spread of the third one but decided to give number four a fair chance.

Listing result (4/4): Advanced Evolution Overview

Juvenile Dungeon Spider Commander	
Evolution Prerequisites	
Species	Juvenile Dungeon Spider
Intellect	> 10

Base	Per level	Attribute
8	1	Health
4	1.5	Body
5	2	Intellect
3	2	Soul

Venom Gland

Secrete a toxic substance from the mandibles that can harm lesser creatures.

Silk Spinning

Secrete a sticky string that can ensnare weaker creatures.

Command Subordinates

Command subordinate members of your organization. They will follow your will as if it were an instinct.

Observation

Obtain System information about a target.

Well, then . . .

The lack of Health and Body screamed at Click to run away and not look back, and the massive increase in Intellect and Soul, while impressive, didn't do too much to push back against those instincts. Click was about to open the third choice again, but one little Skill held their rapt attention.

[Command Subordinates]. The spider instinctively knew that all of their brethren fell under their "organization," and that those spiders *only* acted on instinct. To be able to control that . . .

The System was wrong. There was no *real* choice in the presence of an objectively correct one.

Evolution option selected: Juvenile Dungeon Spider Commander
Beginning evolution . . .

Click's body began to morph, but this time their size remained mostly the same. Instead, something changed deep within them—their internal structure. It didn't hurt. That was all Click could say about the sensation they felt, as if whatever part of them responsible for feeling and comprehending pain *or* pleasure was simply turned off for the time being. As the feeling finally faded, a few new markings and colorations appeared on the spider's abdomen to signify their new authority.

Evolution Carryover bonus obtained!

Juvenile Dungeon Spider (Level 1)

Name	Click
Soul Link	Rockfort Hamlet Dungeon Core [????????]
Classes	N/A

Attributes	
Health	11/11
Body	6
Intellect	156
Soul	5

Skill unlocked: Command Subordinates
Skill unlocked: Observation

> **Level 2: Venom Gland**
> *Secrete a toxic substance from the mandibles that can harm lesser creatures.*

> **Level 8: Silk Spinning**
> *Secrete a sticky string that can ensnare weaker creatures.*

> **Level 1: Command Subordinates**
> *Command subordinate members of your organization. They will follow your will as if it were an instinct.*

> **Level 1: Observation**
> *Obtain System information about a target.*

> **Bonuses**
> Once in a Generation (Intellect) | +150
> Evolution Carryover (Health) | +3
> Evolution Carryover (Body) | +2
> Evolution Carryover (Intellect) | +1
> Evolution Carryover (Soul) | +2

"URRROAAAAHHHHH!" A baleful roar sounded before Click regained their sense of feeling and could properly appreciate their new abilities.

A massive predator, moving on two pairs of thin hair-covered legs extending out of an equally hairy torso, bounded over to Click's old web with its mouth wide open. Sharp teeth gnashed into the webbing—and several spiders. Most spiders were able to escape, despite how densely the swarm was crowded around the web, but the predator quickly readied itself for seconds.

All the while, Click sat far above the action, torn between two choices. The legs on one half of their body were twitching every which way, yet always pointing away from the predator—no matter how swiftly it dashed around the swarm of spiders below—trying to pull

Click in the opposite direction. Those legs were the epitome of fight-or-flight and embodied the fear more strongly than the spider had ever felt: a clawing desperation that would writhe, scream, and pull with the strength of an entire tribe of spiders to get away.

However, they were held in place by Click's other four legs, which were acting very differently. One was dug into the webbing, while another reached out for their eaten brethren. The last two legs shook with promises of violence that the four on the other side knew it wouldn't be able to make good on. But those legs didn't care. They held an ocean of fury for every drop of spider blood shed and stood uncompromisingly with a strength of will to match the snapping maw of the spider-killer below.

While Click wrestled with their choices, they couldn't help but consider their new powers. The predator would always be a threat—watching, hungry. Who was to say Click wouldn't eventually be its next meal? It didn't matter how careful Click was; even as a [Spider Commander] they knew that there were too many variables in the world for them to keep track of. The only thing Click could do was remove some of those variables to make things safer. And now, the spider had a weapon to remove *this* particular variable.

[Command Subordinates]! Click all but shouted the Skill name in their head. *Let's take that thing down!*

CHAPTER EIGHT

Army Commander's First Day on the Job

Notice to all townsfolk,

With the first sign of spring, the bears of the nearby forest have begun to wake from their winter slumber. They may still be in a state of torpor, but that is not to say that they are docile. The long, cold months have eaten away at their internal fat reserves, and they have awakened hungry. Thus, they will be wandering the forest in search of food. While they wander, these creatures are to be considered a threat. They WILL eat you.

Until the bears of the forest fully awaken and satiate themselves, no individual is permitted to wander into the forest on their own, no matter how well-armed and armored they may be. Groups at least three members strong are allowed, so long as they are properly equipped to fight a bear. Numbers are only part of what will ensure survival; if every townsperson fought a bear with naught but their work clothes, we would have to replace all our fields with graves. Likewise, a single person with a fancy sword would merely be a meal holding a toothpick to a bear.

Please be smart! There has been plenty of loss here these past few years. Do not add to our sorrows.

—Notice posted to the Rockfort Hamlet town center's message board; underneath the official-looking document is a request for bear meat from a local farmer

Spiders ran about in absolute pandemonium. A ghastly set of fangs dove into the scrambling throng and made a meal out of whatever it could catch. Throughout it all, none of the overwhelmed arachnids seemed to realize that the safety of home was only a short distance away.

[Command Subordinates]! Click summoned the Skill in their head. It was the first time they'd used an "active" Skill, but doing so was as instinctual as breathing.

Of the spiders clamoring around in the chaos of the predator's sudden appearance, three quickly became rapt with attention.

Wait, only three?

The [Spider Commander] clicked their mandibles once. But it was a start.

The three spiders were behind the quadrupedal attacker and out of its sight. Not having many options, Click commanded the trio to bite at the creature's back left leg with their venomous mandibles.

Of course, the venom didn't kill the attacker, or even wound it, for that matter. But it was distracting enough to make the predator turn its head away from the spiders it *was* about to eat and towards the three that were trying to eat *it* instead. A quick kick threw the trio off and bought the other spiders several seconds.

Click realized that the three spiders thrown off were too far away now to get back into the fight, especially without getting eaten now that they'd made an enemy of the predator. Click decided to try again. *[Command Subordinates]*.

> Skill level up! Command Subordinates (2)

This time, four spiders in the middle of the throng came to attention. Click directed them to spin their webs around the predator's other back paw in an attempt to trip it up.

While the creature was assessing the damage from the first attack by licking its left leg, the four spiders made their way to the large right leg and began to wrap their webbing around the paw. Some went around its shin like a rope while other webbing was matted into its fur, and all of the webs were anchored to the ground or to other rocky features.

The predator finally noticed what was going on and kicked its back right leg. The spiders were thrown off; even worse, the webbing came loose without any kind of effort. Some of it stayed on, however, and the creature bit at it to get the gummy substance out of its fur. Another few seconds were gained.

So, webs can work against it, but they're not strong enough on their own. Click looked away from the fighting for an instant as they heard the buzzing of a small insect flying by, but they quickly refocused on the predator in the distance. *Maybe the web just needs to be big enough? But there's not enough time to spin something like that up.*

Click's mandibles opened in a smile as they looked down at where they were sitting, but then they caught sight of some of the insects stuck in the massive web. The spider was overcome by a sudden wave of emotions and tried to find some sort of balance between them. Was Click going to sacrifice their biggest source of food, or let this predator continue its wanton destruction?

Instincts clashed. Emotions conflicted. The need for food was great, but the drive to live loomed greater. This predator was a threat to not just Click, but the whole spider tribe. The [Spider Commander] didn't care too much for the others, especially with how they'd treated them so far, but both Click and the other spiders were still part of the same tribe. And that meant Click could control them with their Skill to make life easier. Click couldn't just toss that away!

At least, that was how the [Spider Commander] rationalized the instinct to protect and fight for the others.

Now that Click knew what they needed to do, they needed to figure out how to actually do it. The webbing attack brought up the idea that something big enough would be able to harm the predator, but Click wanted to confirm it. The [Spider Commander] invoked the [Command Subordinates] Skill three times in quick succession and was awarded a level up for their efforts.

> Skill level up! Command Subordinates (3)

Each time they invoked the Skill, a small group of spiders stopped running and came to attention. Click could tell which ones reacted through instinct alone. The miniscule squadrons were immediately dispatched to the back left foot of the predator and instructed to bite down as hard as they could.

The creature yowled as it quickly took a step forward to avoid the dozen or so spiders crowding around its irritated leg. Thick, matted fur protected it from most of the bites, but enough was pushed out of the way, or outright pulled out, that at least one spider was able to have their fangs make contact with flesh.

Click began to scurry out of the massive web and make their way to the safety of their white-pillared home, still in full view of the attack. Their home provided the perfect base of operations for directing the others. Once the [Spider Commander] was in the clear, they repeated the same action as before, invoking [Command Subordinates] three times.

This time, fifteen spiders ran up to the webbed-up back leg and bit down hard. The predator let out another scream and took another jump forward, this time slightly towards the right.

Another repeat performance, and the predator was right next to the webbing.

> Skill level up! Command Subordinates (4)

But Click hadn't entirely focused on just moving the creature where they wanted it. The [Spider Commander] commanded another group to tie the webs together tighter and even to cut some down. As it was, the mega-web was spread out thinly enough that if the predator was to jump through it, it might just break through and leave a giant hole instead of getting caught.

The small group of spiders worked together to cut the web loose at the ends and fold it in on itself until it was at least three times as thick. With a little bit of additional reinforcement, the final net was done.

Skill level up! Command Subordinates (5)

Click just needed everyone in the right place. With a few more calls to [Command Subordinates], they were.

And . . . now! Cut and drop! Click screamed the instructions in their head alongside the Skill's activation, and the other spiders responded perfectly.

Skill level up! Command Subordinates (6)

The net fell and fully enveloped the massive creature, binding its legs together as the entire monster went tumbling to the ground with one final yelp.

Click jumped up and down in excitement and ran over to inspect what was now *their* prey. The [Spider Commander] opened their mandibles in a smile, and the other spiders followed suit. Even they realized what had just happened.

But what happened next made Click feel something brand new: self-loathing.

The predator pulled at the webbing several times, and after one particularly forceful tug, managed to break free. It let out an angry scream and began to stomp on the spiders around it, no longer interested in sating its belly. It just wanted to sate its rage.

Flying paws missed Click by mere inches, and they tried to withdraw whatever spiders they could to their home as a last-ditch effort to save the tribe, but their Skill wasn't working properly.

[Command Subordinates].

Only a single spider came to attention, rather than the nine or so that Click had expected.

[Command Subordinates].

[Command Subordinates]!

Nothing. None of the other spiders even bothered to look at Click.

What's happening? Is it stress from the attack? Or maybe I exhausted myself? I don't feel tired, but the Skill might run on something that I can't see or feel that has petered out!

Click's mandibles fell, and they turned around to escape back to their home. The rest of the web spiders might've been done for, but at least the [Spider Commander] could save themself, even though they wanted to try and pull *some* of their brethren along with them to safety. It hurt.

But before Click could move more than an inch, something stopped them.

A loud yowl from the predator rang out—not of rage, but of pain. Click faced the creature again and saw an incomparable sight. A massive spider, larger than all of the other ones there, was on the predator's back and biting down with enormous fangs, which dripped toxic neon blue.

Several other spiders, also new juveniles, jumped up alongside it and bit down onto the predator, making it reel back even more. Within moments, the creature was quickly overpowered and fell back down to the ground. The spider bites didn't stop, and the pitiful thing soon stopped screaming, then stopped moving. It was dead.

The rest of the spiders began to cheer as the largest of the group jumped down and made its way towards Click.

What was that? Who is this new spider? the [Spider Commander] thought frantically. Then they remembered that they had another Skill from their most recent evolution and used it on the large newcomer. *[Observation].*

System Query: Observation Listing Results (1/1): Advanced Overview

Juvenile Alpha Dungeon Spider Hunter (Level 2)	
Soul Link	Rockfort Hamlet Dungeon Core [????????]
Classes	N/A

Evolution Prerequisites	
Species	Juvenile Dungeon Spider
Body	> 20

Attributes	
Health	50
Body	57
Intellect	5
Soul	5

Level 18: Venom Gland *Secrete a toxic substance from the mandibles that can harm lesser creatures.*

Level 1: Silk Spinning *Secrete a sticky string that can ensnare weaker creatures.*

Level 6: Prey Detection *Instinctually sense the location of prey and its movements.*

Level 3: Command Subordinates *Command subordinate members of your organization. They will follow your will as if it were an instinct.*

WHAT?!

Click was without words, and not just because they didn't know how to speak any.

Fifty-seven Body? This is a god amongst spiders, the absolute apex of physical ability among us! Almost all of its Skills are ridiculously high level. And [Command Subordinates]? That jerk stole my Skill!

Well, it probably hadn't stolen their Skill, but Click had found an evolutionary branch that offered it and had taken it against everything their instincts had told them. It was *their* gift! But what kind of evolutions did this newcomer have to go through to get something like *that*?

The massive spider walked over and stopped right before Click. The two looked each other in the eyes, and the [Spider Commander] could feel a sense of familiarity.

The other spider shoved Click out of the way and slowly walked over to their home with a large group of smaller spiders on its tail. All fawning over their savior, no doubt.

Click remembered where they'd met. That was the physically gifted spider that had stolen their food earlier by jumping and grabbing flies out of the air like nobody's business! And now that jerk was apparently in charge . . .

CHAPTER NINE

Bullying Is Wrong

Everyone has a reason why they became an adventurer. Money is one of the most common ones, and a desire to do good is often cited by those with holy Classes. But for some, those who likely would have become soldiers in another life, it could just be out of a love for battle.

Sometimes, adventuring parties might be made up of people with different motivations, but they must always be careful that their motivations do not conflict. And this goes beyond something as simple as everyone being in it for the money and creating rifts when someone wants more of the loot than them. No, this relates to the survival of the party itself.

A priestly Class might wish to give away free healing or divest themselves of the party's resources with no desire for patronage, much to the chagrin of another, more monetarily motivated party member. Such a party is not likely to survive long, as its members would be motivated to split in order to preserve what each of them finds most important.

But what of the one who loves battle? They may rush into

*a fight they have little chance of winning—or worse, into
a fight they know they can survive but the other members
would not—even if the designated team leader or strategist
demands they disengage. Such a party will not last long, as
its individual members are not likely to last long. See the
harrowing tale of Sir Jenkins for a more extreme example.*

*The point is that when forming an adventuring party,
make sure not only that the composition of your combat abilities is complementary, but also that your motivations are.
Make sure that you can all live with your teammates' desires,
and make sure you will live if they obtain them.*

**—Excerpt from *What They Don't Tell You About
Adventuring* by Milford Bandernickle**

A strong arm rammed into Click and sent them airborne.

Click felt the world around them spin as they flew backwards, only to quickly meet the cold ground in a muted, yet stinging thud. They waved their arms around as if in great pain.

You call that a shove? That predator had a stronger arm, and you some-how killed it! I bet it only died because it couldn't stand how weak you are.

Click slowly righted themself, fighting off minor disorientation, and bowed their head in supplication to the [Alpha Hunter].

Wow, you're such an idiot. You can't even tell that I don't actually mean it!

The act of deference sufficiently pleased it, and the larger spider walked away, out of the white-pillared home in search of a fight.

Because that was all it was: an act.

This had been Click's life for the past week. Ever since the larger spider had evolved into that rare form, it had essentially taken control of the entire tribe and used its position to bully Click. Not that the [Spider Commander] could entirely blame it; Click posed the biggest threat to its authority. No, wait. Click *totally* could blame it for being so mean! But they were also at least grateful that the larger spider had decided to keep Click alive.

But that wasn't an act of mercy on the [Alpha Hunter]'s part. Click proved their usefulness by commanding the web spiders to create more web traps in their part of the cave, which had brought a large amount of extra food to the tribe. That, combined with their shows of submission, had the [Alpha Hunter] thinking that Click was more useful to it alive.

And what an idiot it is for that! Click lifted their mandibles into a wide smile—so wide and scrunched up that it could be considered smug. The [Spider Commander] realized that since their rival didn't have the [Observation] Skill, it was limited to its intuition and physical observations of the world around it to guess how Click felt.

What a wonderful idea, performing an action that doesn't match at all how I feel! I can't believe nobody else is doing it, but they probably haven't figured it out. It's so easy to make the [Alpha Hunter] believe I'm meek and under its control when I couldn't care less about it!

Click watched as a massive group of about fifty hunter spiders followed their leader out into the cave, a mix of regular juveniles alongside a few juvenile hunters. Several of the spiders had evolved over the past few days, catching up to the number of evolutionary transformations that Click and the [Alpha Hunter] had undergone. Those that had evolved only enjoyed an improvement to what they were already able to do and hadn't gained anything like Click and the [Alpha Hunter] had. Still, they seemed pretty satisfied with the hands they had been dealt and continued on with their lives.

And with their rival's prying eyes turned somewhere else and all the hunters gone, Click was ready to do the same. With a series of massive leaps, the spider bounced across several stalagmites and made their way to the tribe's communal webbing. Several of the evolved web spiders greeted *their* leader with a wave, and the [Spider Commander] returned the gesture. The regular juveniles simply ignored Click and continued their silent vigil for food. Click felt that the biggest benefit of evolution was that it gave their brethren just enough intelligence to actually use their brains.

All of the spiders were positioned evenly across a single mega-web that stretched across a large section of the cave wall. To get around the mindless, instinct-driven competition, Click had all of the spiders work together on a single web. If a part of the web got filled with enough insects, the spiders wouldn't all flock and fight over the food and would instead stay where they were. After all, those high-density spots weren't part of *their* web; it was everyone's web. And that wasn't all. Since everyone had contributed to the structure, any captures rewarded shared Experience to the entire group!

Click would be lying if they said they hadn't thought of using this to train their own little army to take down the [Alpha Hunter]. But alas, even with a higher [Command Subordinates] Skill and authority over all of the highly leveled web spiders, the web slingers' combat abilities still paled in comparison to their hunter counterparts.

It wouldn't be a fight. It would be a slaughter.

[Command Subordinates], Click called out as they mentally focused on several of the regular juveniles.

The smaller spiders quickly came to attention and waved at their commander.

Skill level up! Command Subordinates (14)

Click had been practicing the Skill over the past few days, and its description had even changed once it had reached level ten. It was now able to work on specific targets rather than a grab bag of whatever happened to be close by.

And that wasn't all; [Venom Gland] had also gone up significantly, though not as much. Apparently, the bugs caught in the tribe's webbing made valid targets for the Skill and eating them had gotten Click's Skill up to level seven. And the general Experience obtained from those catches and kills brought the spider itself up to level nine. The [Spider Commander] made ample use of their Skills whenever they got the chance, as long as the [Alpha Hunter] wasn't nearby.

And, speaking of the devil, a chittering came from the distance and the leader of the tribe came running back with about fifteen hunter spiders in tow. Right on their tails was a trio of large predators, each much larger than the one that had attacked last week.

The group of spiders made it back to their white-pillared home and found refuge in the barrier. One of the creatures pawed at it with a low growl, but eventually turned around and left.

The hunter spiders of the group didn't celebrate, however. They carried with them several insects, most already half-eaten. They'd gone on what was supposed to be a hunting trip, but the sudden attack had ended it early. That was happening a lot recently.

That was also the real reason why the [Alpha Hunter] was keeping Click around. The [Spider Commander] could control the web spiders and make them much more efficient than they would be otherwise. With the repeated bad hunting trips, the rest of the tribe would need the output from the webs to make up for their failures. And with fewer and fewer hunters returning, Click's efforts were the only thing keeping everyone fed.

Click asked themself why they didn't simply leave for greener pastures, why they didn't just let all of the fools back home die of starvation while they lived the easy life. The spider could never come up with a concrete answer. Maybe it was some kind of emotional attachment to their home, or maybe loyalty towards their brethren?

Click convinced themself it was because it gave them the best chance at survival given their skillset. What use was [Command Subordinates] without anyone to command? At least here Click had *some* spiders to order around, even if they were mostly just stationary web spiders.

Of course, Click tried to command some of the hunter spiders as well in order to boost the webs' output, but that didn't go so well. Even the [Alpha Hunter] wasn't so stupid as to let Click have control over the tribe's military. The first time Click tried to control some of the hunters, the leader had tried tossing Click out into a pack of predators. That, thankfully, had failed when the creatures tried going after the [Alpha Hunter] instead of the [Spider Commander].

Click didn't think that the predators' behavior was just a coincidence, though. The creature that the [Alpha Hunter] had killed earlier was much smaller than the ones attacking now, and *those* predators didn't seem to be interested in the spiders for food.

They just wanted blood.

Maybe the smaller predator was a child of the ones attacking or belonged to their tribe. Click knew that the spiders' parent had given its life to feed everyone. So perhaps that kind of parental instinct to care for one's young was common beyond just spiders, and different species just had a different way of expressing it. The predators were expressing it by wanting revenge on the spider that had killed their child.

Click grabbed a quick bite and then left the mega-web, heading towards a small alcove away from the others. The [Alpha Hunter] would be heading up the web to get a meal after its most recent failure, anyway, and it wouldn't do any good for Click to stick around.

The remote hidey hole gave an ample view of the entrance to the mega-web, while still technically being part of it. Small bits of jagged rock jutted out of the alcove, which bit into Click's abdomen, but they ignored it. The safety the spot provided trumped any and all minor discomforts.

The [Alpha Hunter] entered the massive web and rather than grab at the nearest morsel, made its way to the center of the structure. Helpless insects lay all around it, mindlessly squirming against the silk without realizing they were captured. The head spider ignored them.

With a thought, the leader activated a Skill several times, and three dozen web spiders all around it came to attention. A foreign [Command Subordinates] washed over Click and didn't do so much as tickle them. Apparently, neither spider was "under" the other, despite their differing opinions on the matter.

The [Alpha Hunter] jumped down from the web into the ranks of its hunting party, and the other spiders under its spell followed.

Wait. Were they . . .

The large spider raised its mandibles into a smile, something akin to a dumb and toothy grin, and led the fifty or so web and hunter spiders back into the deeper parts of the cave.

That idiot! Click all but screamed in their head as they quickly emerged from their alcove. The jagged stones bit into their skin, but they didn't pay it any mind.

> 1 Damage taken! Health: 22/23

Click brushed the notification off while red filled their eyes. Something far worse was going on. They seethed as they processed what had happened.

The [Alpha Hunter] doesn't even care about having access to food or the rest of the tribe; it just wants to hunt! Why else would it ignore the food here? What good are a bunch of web spiders going to be in a fight? They've barely even used their fangs, and their venom Skills are still close to level one!

The [Spider Commander] clicked their mandibles together in a sharp snap.

On the other hand, it could be doing this because putting me in charge of the entire tribe's food supply would give me more power than it would be comfortable with, but is it really intelligent enough to understand something like that? No, that's not it. That idiot just can't stop hunting.

Its addiction is going to be the end of this tribe if I don't do something about it. It's time to take the alpha out.

CHAPTER TEN

Solo Reconnaissance Mission

The biggest mistake a warrior, general, or even adventurer can make is thinking that levels determine everything. After all, everyone has had it drilled into their heads from an early age that levels mean everything. Schools assign grades based on levels earned, entire careers are restricted to those with the right Classes and attributes, to name some examples.

However, they are not entirely wrong; higher levels and the right System makeup can provide many advantages, but that view is still limited. A single advantage does not win a battle, let alone a war.

If a level five Swordsman went up against one who was level six, most would immediately jump in to point out that the level six fighter would win. But what if the level five fighter had a more powerful weapon? Then those same people might complain that money creates an uneven playing field.

So now I ask: what would happen if the level five Swordsman ambushed the level six? Or fought with the sun behind them? Or prevented their opponent from getting a restful night's sleep?

Anyone who would complain about an uneven playing field now is an idiot. True battles, wars, are never fair! You make use of every advantage you can get if you don't want to end up dead! String up the corpses of their children if you have to. As long as you and your soldiers go home, anything is fair!

—Excerpt from a guest lecture at the Shostran Royal Military Academy by General Montgomery Fairwind, one year before being tried and executed for war crimes

Click sat on a tall stalagmite that extended far enough into the air to give them a 360-degree view of most of the cave, and it was more than enough to keep track of their target. Two days of near-constant surveillance gave the [Spider Commander] plenty of information to generate an idea of how the [Alpha Hunter] operated.

That big jerk was an idiot, but Click wasn't; the [Spider Commander] knew that a direct confrontation would lead to inevitable death, so there they stood, trying to better understand their enemy.

In the far distance, the [Alpha Hunter]'s party of fifty lesser spiders made quick work of any fly or other insect they came across. There had been a swarm of them recently, most of them around the remains of the predator the leader had slain, which had rotted too much for even the hungriest of spiders to make a meal out of. While the air was thick with bugs, Click could make out a visible path carved through the omnipresent swarm where the [Alpha Hunter] had been. For such an idiot, it was at least effective.

Click was tempted to grab one of the flies out of the air for a quick snack, but a loud noise in the distance grabbed their attention.

"URROAAHHH!"

A lone predator howled as the [Alpha Hunter] leapt onto its back and bit down hard with venomous fangs, piercing fur and skin alike, as the creature contorted its body in an attempt to shake off the attacking spider. The [Alpha Hunter] simply performed a backflip and landed on its eight legs on the cavern floor without a care or concern in the world.

Pfft, show-off.

The other spiders tried to follow suit. They didn't have as much success individually, but who needed to do things perfectly with an army? The large numbers swarmed the predator and pushed it even further on the defensive.

The creature kicked off most of the spiders and flattened the few that remained on its fur against the nearby stalagmites, but it didn't try to run despite it being clear that it wouldn't win the fight. It just took a few steps back and repositioned itself, letting loose another howl every few seconds.

What is it—ah, that's what!

All of a sudden, three more predators jumped into the fray from out of nowhere. Even on the rocky tower, Click didn't see where they came from or when they arrived. Black fur billowed as the trio blurred onto the battlefield, fangs bared, eyes filled with piercing hatred.

They all launched themselves at the [Alpha Hunter] at once, ignoring the forty smaller spiders. The lead spider effortlessly jumped out of the way, making use of its comparatively smaller size to avoid fang and paw alike.

The fight went on for half a minute, and none of the predators could land a hit on the lead spider. The [Alpha Hunter], on the other hand, applied plenty of envenomed bites to the predators, though none of them seemed to be showing any effects from the toxin running through their veins. In fact, it was the [Alpha Hunter] who was beginning to slow.

Wham! A speeding paw slammed into the lead spider and sent it flying into a nearby rock. One of its legs was bent out of shape, and it struggled to get back up. The fight should've been over, but . . .

The [Alpha Hunter] straightened itself out and ran back into the fray, but it was far away and took time to return to the battle. Click stared at the idiot, too shocked to even think about how it had managed to stay alive for so long. In the meantime, the predators took the opportunity to thin the enemy herd and began to eat or step on the various spiders around them.

Click's brethren put up a valiant effort to defend themselves; the hunter spiders gave their all in the fight. Curiously, though, some of the web spiders that the [Alpha Hunter] had dragged along began to spin webs where they stood and launched them at the predators. The attacks didn't do much, but the few that hit vulnerable spots, such as the eyes, worked as somewhat effective distractions. Too bad they weren't effective enough.

As the spider death toll began to climb, a few members of the group began shaking. After witnessing the death of one of their brethren, the nearby spiders would begin to shiver as well. The chain continued until spiders that hadn't seen a drop of blood were beginning to shiver also, as long as they were surrounded by enough of their jittery brethren.

By the time the [Alpha Hunter] had returned, the entire group was shivering, and the lead spider began to mimic them too. Something in that motion pulled forth a deeply buried instinct and made the [Alpha Hunter]—that battle-junkie idiot—do the unthinkable: it turned around and ran.

The [Alpha Hunter] ran back to its white-pillared home and didn't even look back as the rest of the spider swarm followed. The predators tried to catch it, but it was too deft and easily evaded their attacks as if empowered by some new energy solely dedicated to fleeing.

Click pushed back at a rising instinct to run back home as well but held fast, and the sensation eventually faded. Click's distance from the fight was probably why the instinct wasn't as strong, but if it could make a bloodthirsty fool like the [Alpha Hunter] flee, then it must have been nearly irresistible over there.

What was that? It was definitely some kind of instinct, that's for sure. But something so powerful? It makes no sense.

Click imagined facing one of the predators and felt the urge to run back home just from the thought alone.

It looks like that particular instinct triggers when a hunting party is about to face total annihilation. That also makes sense, as it would keep at least some of us alive to live and fight another day. The [Alpha Hunter] was beginning to slow down by the end of the battle against four adult predators; it definitely would've died if it weren't for that instinct . . .

Click's mind was immediately abuzz with thoughts, plans, and schemes. Here was a weakness, a surefire way to get rid of that idiot once and for all! But there were so many safeguards in place to prevent that from happening. The [Spider Commander] would just have to perform some sabotage.

Time for Some . . . Sabotage!

Where can a spy do the most damage? According to common sense, it would be as a figure of authority. A commander in an army can purposefully position their own troops to lose or to allow an enemy to pass by with little resistance. But such a defeat would be suspicious. Would not those above them question that level of incompetence and surmise that it was purposeful?

According to another voice, those boorish romance novels young women are so fond of reading these days, it would be as the lover of someone with authority. Someone who could subtly convince the ones in charge to make poor decisions and have all the suspicion fall on the innocent lover instead of the true threat. But any thorough investigation would eventually uncover the spy, and they would be executed, along with their naive lover. Funnily enough, this literary trend has actually reduced the number of extra-marital relationships nobles have taken up recently, out of fear of something that almost never happens.

But the true best place for a spy to do the most damage

happens to be as a commoner. Sure, they may not have great authority, but at the same time, nobody will be looking for them. Nestled in amongst a large population, they can subtly influence the masses to wreak havoc while melting back into the crowds to prevent detection. An angry mob is easy to whip up, and it is quite difficult to try hundreds of people in court at once.

Of course, such a position requires skill and tact to truly make the most of, but this program will train you to do so. There's a whole kingdom up north that is ripe for you to sow all sorts of chaos.

—Meeting notes from the Johovian Spy Network, one month before its post-war eradication

The [Alpha Hunter] strutted onto the tribe's web and called out to all of the nearby spiders. Many web spiders answered the call, from basic juveniles, who operated solely on instinct, to their more evolved forms, who were at best just cannon fodder—or at worst, a burden. But that wasn't all. One of the more woefully unqualified spiders to answer the call to arms was, interestingly, Click.

The lead spider regarded its diminutive rival with the equivalent of trepidation. A little bit of bowing and pleading later and the [Alpha Hunter] forgot its concerns. It most likely believed that this was an opportunity to rid itself of its greatest competition. In all honesty, with the risk Click was taking to make their plan a reality, it really was a possibility. But one that was worth it.

The hunt went surprisingly smoothly. The fifty-strong group remained entirely unmolested for an incredibly long time. Click was even able to let loose their own hunter spider instincts, which they otherwise kept suppressed, and find some release in doing what they were born for. It helped that the [Alpha Hunter] hadn't bothered to steal any of Click's kills like it had so long ago. In fact, Click hadn't seen that idiot for the past few minutes; where could it have gone off to?

"URROAAHHH!"

Oh, that's where.

The lead spider had gone off on its own in search of more "worthy" prey, and it had found just that. It was currently in a fight against a lone predator, which was reminiscent of one from the previous big fight. And just like that last melee, the [Alpha Hunter] was making an absolute chump out of its opponent.

Some of the hunter spiders and the more battle-hardened web spiders attempted to help out, while the newly recruited web spiders stayed put. Click couldn't blame them and even joined them in their inactivity.

But the [Alpha Hunter] didn't seem to care about who was helping or who wasn't and continued to pummel the poor creature. It let out another howl but didn't try to flee the battle.

Click's eyes went wide as they realized what the predator was trying to do. The [Spider Commander] quickly turned around in a circle in search of any sign of movement, be it through sound, sight, or even smell.

There was nothing. But that didn't mean there really *was* nothing. The spider understood how skilled their opponents were and wasn't about to let themself be caught in what was coming. Click surveyed their surroundings for a hiding spot. Sadly, there wasn't much beyond a small alcove underneath a very large rock, but it would have to do. The [Spider Commander] took their place there.

As if on cue, a new trio of predators jumped into the fray and began to tear apart the smaller spiders. The predators killed at least a dozen or so before realizing that the [Alpha Hunter] was still locked in battle against the lone scout. They switched targets.

But that wasn't before one of the spiders in the group began shaking. The sensation spread to the one next to it, but Click reacted before it could go any further than that.

[Command Subordinates]! the small spider shouted in their mind and targeted the two that were being taken by instinct. That instinct was suddenly overridden by the Skill, and something new commanded the spiders.

Click mentally ordered the shivering duo to still themselves, and they did. If the [Alpha Hunter] could override a web spider's instincts towards hunting, the [Spider Commander] should be able to override a spider's instinct towards fleeing! And they did.

Click's eyes slowly peeked out from their little hidey-hole before quickly ducking back out of sight. *Why couldn't I be somewhere safer, like a stalagmite? Or home? Or just not here? Oh, that's right. My Skill doesn't work at that range. Sure, it can stretch to cover an entire battlefield like this one, but only when I'm part of it. That's dumb! The Skill isn't made for fighters, so why does it expect me to be one to use it?!*

Back in the fray, another lucky hit sent the [Alpha Hunter] flying, and the predators began to slaughter the rest of the hunting pack.

Click, still sitting in their little bunker, tightened their focus and fired off a barrage of Skill invocations as the wave of death brought forth the spiders' primal instincts.

[Command Subordinates]! A trio that had all begun to shake at once were immediately quieted, along with six more surrounding them. Click removed their control and all nine began to fight once more.

[Command Subordinates]! The corpse of a spider was chewed up and thrown into the throng, coating over a dozen others in blood and guts, most of them web spiders. Click had them cover up the body in silk so that the others would not be able to make out the level of gore.

[Command Subordinates]! No instances of shaking that time around, but Click felt the lead spider was simply taking too long to return to the battle and directed one of the others to lead a predator over to it.

Skill level up! Command Subordinates (16)

The battle continued, and while the predators almost entirely focused on the [Alpha Hunter], the rest of the hunting party faced continuously climbing casualty rates. Eventually, there were only three spiders left, and even though they began to shiver, their leader ignored them. It wasn't the critical mass required to override the alpha's own bloodlust, and now it wouldn't ever be.

More sharp bites and flying claws, even more jukes and dodges, but all of them were growing sloppy. Things were beginning to slow down as the [Alpha Hunter] slowly burned through its steam. The predators sensed this, as well as the renewed lack of intention to flee. The previously lone scout began to go after the remaining spiders.

Click looked at them and felt a strange pang of emotion. They were being dragged to their deaths for Click's gain, and something about the situation didn't sit well with them. Whatever that feeling was, Click shook it off with the understanding that they would've died eventually otherwise. If not as part of this hunting party, then as part of another one. The [Spider Commander] still threw one more [Command Subordinates] in the spiders' direction to have them flee to safety.

It was too bad that their path ran right next to Click's little alcove; a lone predator in pursuit caught the scent of one last spider. Click swore, or at least did the spider equivalent of telling themself off. Seeing the paw right in front of them triggered Click's fight-or-flight instinct, and in such an enclosed space with no escape, the [Spider Commander] was faced with a terrible choice. They knew the answer, but their entire being screamed to make the wrong one. But maybe with enough willpower, they could keep still and . . .

> Skill level up! Venom Gland (8)

Whoops . . .

The predator yowled at the bite on their nose before tackling the rock and pushing it away with a rage-fueled howl. The [Spider Commander] was completely exposed with no other spiders to command.

Click jumped to the side as angry fangs came crashing down. They barely managed to jump out of the way when a speeding paw struck their back and sent them flying.

> 7 Damage taken! Health: 15/23

An entire third?!

A flash of pain exploded from almost every point on Click's body. Several of their legs screamed in agony, and one of them was entirely unresponsive. Ichor leaked out of the spider's abdomen at a slow rate, but they couldn't properly gauge the severity of the injury from feeling alone—the fear they were feeling was too acute—but the arachnid didn't need to.

Click didn't understand numbers, but proportions were a trivial concept. And they could very well wrap their head around the idea that if they got hit like that twice more, they would most certainly die. And with the mass of black fur running towards them, that reality was approaching quickly.

The [Spider Commander] fought through the blaring pain alarms sounding in their head and thought for a moment about how they were going to get out of this. They couldn't beat the predator in a straight up fight, especially not alone, and they had no chance of getting away either. The only spider that *could* do either of those was . . .

A brilliant idea popped into Click's head. A brilliant and downright *terrible* idea.

[Command Subordinates]! There were no other lesser spiders on the battlefield left to command. But there was . . .

The Skill failed, but Click hadn't: [Command Subordinates] wasn't able to take control of the [Alpha Hunter], but it had most certainly caught its attention. And it was pissed.

The lead spider jumped out of its three-on-one battle and ran towards the [Spider Commander] with absolute hatred in its eyes. It even beat out the predator that was about to leap onto Click, pushing the predator off balance.

Click did the only thing it could against the [Alpha Hunter] and bowed in supplication. That didn't help this time, and the larger spider struck with all of its might. The [Spider Commander] went flying again, and when they landed, they suffered a nasty hit.

4 Damage taken! Health: 11/23

Sure, so now *you realize I'm not actually sorry!*

Honestly, it wasn't as bad as getting hit by a predator, but Click was still more than halfway to death. That didn't sit well.

But what did sit well was how the gloating figure of the [Alpha Hunter] became a prime target for the rest of the predators. The predator's attack that had been meant for Click ended up hitting the larger spider instead as sharp fangs dug into its chitinous carapace and lifted it up.

The predator shook its head in a frenzy before throwing the [Alpha Hunter] into the air. Without any kind of built-up webbing Skills or any other specific biological advantage, the spider was completely unable to maneuver as it sailed through the cave and into the jaws of another predator.

Another hard bite, shake, and throw, another catch and repeat. Each time the fangs sunk into the [Alpha Hunter] it must have taken at least a dozen in damage. And with only fifty Health, plus whatever it would've gained in the last week through level ups, it wouldn't be long before . . .

Thud.

The corpse of the [Alpha Hunter] landed on the ground, completely torn to shreds. The predators didn't stop and continued to desecrate the body until it was nothing more than a horribly mangled pile. They turned it into an impromptu litter box as a final act of disrespect to their sworn enemy.

The creatures let out a loud howl, one that lasted longer than any Click had heard them utter before. The predators were joined by many others throughout the cave.

Under the cover of the predators' final battle cry, Click slumped back towards home, towards the protection of the white pillars. After all, it was the dawn of a new era. They would be the one in charge of the tribe now, and the tribe would thrive under them.

> Experience +50 | Next Level: 107/90
> Level up!

Juvenile Dungeon Spider Commander (Level 10)	
Name	Click
Soul Link	Rockfort Hamlet Dungeon Core [????????]
Classes	N/A

Attributes	
Health (+1)	25/25
Body (+1)	19
Intellect (+2)	164
Soul (+2)	23

Level requirement achieved for evolution

Choices available: Dungeon Web Spider, Dungeon Hunter Spider, Dungeon Ambush Trapper Spider, Dungeon Spider Commander

Please select an option

CHAPTER TWELVE

All Hail the King, Baby!

Picking a Class can be quite the challenge, since you need to have made up your mind about what you want, as well as know the best way to get there.

Maybe your strength lies in your skill with numbers, so the [Accountant] or rare [Mathematician] Class would look the most appealing. But if you will be working in a business, then such Classes might not be any good for helping you with what the business actually does. How helpful is only being good with numbers to a bakery?

You might think that it would be easier to pick a Class for a combat-oriented role if you are hoping to become a soldier, mercenary, or adventurer. Simply choosing [Swordsman] or [Archer] based on what weapons you feel most comfortable with should be enough, right? Perhaps when starting out, but what about when your Class evolves? Would a [Monster Scout] or [Counter-Duelist] do better in a fight against a dungeon spider that has no sword to counter? How about in an open battlefield against a soldier?

Learning which Class best suits your needs is the first

step. The second is to learn how to get that Class. The rarest and most powerful of them have all sorts of prerequisites that require a lifetime of dedication to achieve, so it's best to start early. Or be like those who discovered them in the first place and get extremely lucky.

—Excerpt from Chapter 1 of *Classes and You: Finding Your Path through Life*

You can't really expect me to make a choice with just a name. Give me the details! Click said to the voice in their head. It was time for another evolution, and the spider had no intention of picking anything based on instinct alone.

System query received. Producing result . . .   Listing result (1/4): Advanced Evolution Overview

Dungeon Web Spider

Evolution Prerequisites

Species	Any Juvenile Dungeon Spider subspecies

Base	Per level	Attribute
15	1.5	Health
8	1.5	Body
5	2	Intellect
5	1.5	Soul

Venom Gland

Secrete a toxic substance from the mandibles that can harm lesser creatures.

Silk Spinning

Secrete a sticky string that can ensnare weaker creatures.

> **Weaver's Domain**
> *Instinctively know the identity and position of anything on the web.*

The evolution looked like a slightly upgraded version of the original Juvenile Dungeon Web Spider, with a few increased attributes and a new Skill in Weaver's Domain. Why such a Skill wasn't there for the juvenile variant, Click didn't know, but they weren't interested in losing everything they had just to satisfy their mild curiosity.

Next.

> Listing result (2/4): Advanced Evolution Overview

Dungeon Hunter Spider	
Evolution Prerequisites	
Species	Any Juvenile Dungeon Spider subspecies

Base	**Per level**	**Attribute**
20	3	Health
15	3	Body
2	1	Intellect
3	1.5	Soul

> **Venom Gland**
> *Secrete a toxic substance from the mandibles that can harm lesser creatures.*

> **Silk Spinning**
> *Secrete a sticky string that can ensnare weaker creatures.*

> **Prey Detection**
> *Instinctually sense the location of prey and its movements.*

Same as before, it was an upgraded version of the juvenile variant. And it was entirely focused on Body and Health, which Click wasn't particularly interested in. What reason was there to increase either of those attributes if they weren't going to get hit in the first place?

The [Spider Commander] tried to flex one of their legs, but the limb had gone limp. Well, maybe that wasn't quite the case . . .

Listing result (3/4): Advanced Evolution Overview

Dungeon Ambush Trapper Spider

Evolution Prerequisites

Species	Any Juvenile Dungeon Spider subspecies
Skill: Venom Gland	> Level 5
Skill: Silk Spinning	> Level 5

Base	Per level	Attribute
15	3	Health
10	2.5	Body
3	2	Intellect
3	1.5	Soul

Venom Gland
Secrete a toxic substance from the mandibles that can harm lesser creatures.

Silk Spinning
Secrete a sticky string that can ensnare weaker creatures.

Web Launch
Hold and throw your webbing.

It was the exact same as with the other evolution choices, but the prerequisites looked a little different: Skill requirements had increased from level one to level five. Maybe it was to make sure every aspect of the evolution was being used to some extent? It would keep spiders who didn't suit the evolution from continuing with it, which sounded like a nice workaround for badly suited instincts.

Click thought back to their own urge to chase bugs down but shook those feelings away. They didn't need the System to tell them what they were good at! Click could do that themself!

Listing result (4/4): Advanced Evolution Overview

Dungeon Spider Commander

Evolution Prerequisites

Species	Any Juvenile Dungeon Spider subspecies
Intellect	> 20
Skill: Command Subordinates	> Level 10

Base	Per level	Attribute
10	2	Health
5	1.5	Body
10	3	Intellect
5	2.5	Soul

Venom Gland

Secrete a toxic substance from the mandibles that can harm lesser creatures.

Silk Spinning

Secrete a sticky string that can ensnare weaker creatures.

Command Subordinates

Command subordinate members of your organization. They will follow your will as if it were an instinct.

Observation

Obtain System information about a target.

There isn't that much difference between this and my current evolution other than bigger numbers. It's still better than all of the other choices. And who knows, maybe the evolution after this one will be even better? But whether or not that's the case, was there ever any doubt about what I would decide on?

Click lifted their mandibles into a smile and made their choice. The prerequisites were quite demanding, but the spider had earned more than enough to meet them.

Evolution option selected: Dungeon Spider Commander
Beginning evolution . . .

Back in the spiders' white-pillared home, nobody noticed as Click returned from their triumphant hunting trip.

The [Spider Commander] walked over to the nearest of their brethren and waved their arms in front of its eyes. It gave them a dismissive look and walked away. The next few spiders Click tried to interact with all behaved the same way.

Huh? Why don't they acknowledge me as their new leader? They don't even recognize me as the second-in-command!

Click ran over to the next spider and began to jump up and down in front of it, even keeping themself in front of it when it tried to turn away. They were definitely getting somewhere, as the other spider lifted a leg and—

Click staggered back a few steps but caught themself quickly. They'd been shoved. Click's eyes burned with a wicked rage.

[Command Subordinates]!

The spiders that had previously ignored them all snapped to attention, their limbs flailing as they were pulled over to Click, mere puppets to the [Spider Commander]'s whims.

The spiders bowed low, but Click could only see the first row of their subordinates. The [Spider Commander] immediately realized the problem: they didn't even come up to half the height of the other spiders. The evolution had shrunk Click and nobody even believed they were the new leader! Click released their control and walked up to the first of their brethren.

The other spiders threw baleful looks at Click before slowly turning around and getting back to whatever they had been doing beforehand. Click was grateful that the others didn't try to take revenge for their embarrassment at coming to attention. The [Spider Commander] would have to fix this.

Several minutes later, after making sure the area truly was clear of predators, Click came back home with the corpse of the [Alpha Hunter] dragging behind them. They had found the original site of its death and dug through layers of soil and dung to retrieve it, but it was absolutely worth it.

The other spiders walked over of their own volition as Click climbed on top of the corpse of the tribe's old leader. Several web spiders from up above also came down, motioning for the rest of the spiders to join in.

Click raised their mandibles and front two arms into the sky. The other spiders did the opposite, lowering the fronts of their bodies down to the ground in deep bows.

It was official now.

All hail Click!

CHAPTER THIRTEEN

Whipping Everyone into Shape

The phrase "standing on the shoulders of giants" refers to how the grand achievements of the Noble Races can be attributed to the work and achievements of our ancestors. Their efforts paved the way for us to rise to such great heights, and it is their shoulders we stand on to reach them.

But there is a corollary to that: those who do not appreciate the work or sacrifices of those before them are doomed to fail. An apprentice blacksmith who does not appreciate the techniques discovered by the metalworkers before them will not be able to forge a proper blade.

It sounds like madness for a skilled worker to ignore something so important. What could be the cause? Sheer arrogance and nothing more.

I would like to bring your attention to recent happenings in the royal court. Our new king, recently ascendant after the "mysterious" death of his father, worked hard to undo all of His work in the kingdom! The nobility grew so much during that era and expanded their glory past the borders of our fair lands too. Our holdings and industrial output expanded tremendously when laborers were made to work more than twelve hours in the day, and now the prince seeks to undo it! What could be the reason for that?

—Public speech given by Lord Avarician Fringe in the Shostran capital, just before being attacked by an angry mob

Click was grateful for everything the [Alpha Hunter] had done. Well, almost everything. It had united the dungeon spiders into a single tribe and made a mark on the rest of the cavern they all called home. And now that tribe was Click's. The new lead spider couldn't help but appreciate the shoulders of the giant they stood on.

The [Spider Commander] stomped on the corpse of the big bully they were currently atop and addressed the crowd of spiders below them. Though there wasn't much "addressing" that could be done. Click waved their arms and mandibles about, and the others simply looked back, a few even trying to copy the movements.

Click snapped their mandibles together in a sharp *click*.

This is hopeless, the spider thought to themself.

"*URRROAAAAHHHHH!*" came a terrible roar from the distance.

A group of predators came rushing in, fury evident in their eyes. They made a beeline for the spiders' white-pillared home, and while Click knew the defensive cage would hold against an assault, they still jumped back in surprise at the impact.

The [Spider Commander] tumbled down from the corpse of the [Alpha Hunter] and barely managed to avoid a paw. The claws attached to the appendage gripped onto the dead [Alpha Hunter] and dragged it out of its old home, but not before a particularly brave—or foolhardy— hunter spider leapt up and bit the paw as it made its egress. Another predator quickly grabbed the corpse with its teeth before another spider could attack and slowly began to walk away with it. The other predators followed along closely behind their leader.

Did they want to keep it as a prize? Click wondered. *Or maybe they don't want it to go back to its old home? Home is safe, and they would not want something they hate to be safe.*

Either way, the brief attack made something very clear to the [Spider Commander]. The war against these predators might have been over, but the spiders still weren't safe. Something would have to be done about that. Click called up [Observation] while looking at one of the departing creatures.

Skill level up! Observation (2)

The spider scolded themself for not doing this earlier; it would've reduced some of the risks of their coup if they had known what these powerful enemies were capable of.

System Query: Observation
Listing Results (1/1): Advanced Overview

Dungeon Hound (Level 8)

Soul Link	Rockfort Hamlet Dungeon Core [????????]
Classes	N/A

Evolution Prerequisites

Species	Juvenile Dungeon Hound

Attributes	
Health	150
Body	69
Intellect	20
Soul	35

Level 7: Iron Fangs
Teeth are reinforced to be harder and sharper.

> **Level 5: Pack Tactics**
> *Instinctively understand the desires of the rest of the pack.*

> **Level 6: Prey Detection**
> *Instinctually sense the location of prey and its movements.*

Click was taken aback by the high attribute numbers, especially for Body. These predators, the dungeon hounds, likely had their size advantage to thank. But then, the [Alpha Hunter] had had a similarly high Body attribute, and it was downright miniscule in comparison!

And [Pack Tactics]. The [Spider Commander] looked back to their tribe. *I wish I had a Skill like that. I don't think any of the others can actually understand me. Only what their instincts tell them. Wait . . .*

It was a longshot, but Click called up and considered the description of [Command Subordinates] again. Words were still something they didn't quite understand, but they didn't need to with the way the System supplied information to them.

> **Level 15: Command Subordinates**
> *Command subordinate members of your organization. They will follow your will as if it were an instinct. Can target specific subordinates to command.*

"Follow my will as if it were instinct," Click quoted. *In that case, [Command Subordinates]!*

A quartet of web spiders snapped to attention and looked at their leader intently as Click supplied a series of instructions. After a few seconds, the four spiders quickly ran up to the web mega-structure and began to weave a long, ladder-like tunnel back down to their white-pillared home.

It wasn't a complex task, all things considered, but it wasn't something they would do normally.

Climb up to the big web.

Weave a web in the shape of a tube back down to here.

Perform the above two steps again, but with enough space added between this tube and the previous one so that it goes through a different gap between the white pillars.

Those were the instructions Click had given. And seeing how the quartet continued to weave new pillars coming down from the mega-web, it seemed that the Skill *could* impart complex instructions beyond native instincts.

But as far as the [Spider Commander] knew, the Skill was just for giving short-term orders. Could its instructions last beyond the Skill's active effect?

Click regarded the spiders with a smile after they completed their task. Their brethren smiled back, and Click made sure the reaction was genuine by deactivating whatever trace of [Command Subordinates] was left. Their mandibles didn't lower.

That only made Click smile wider, seeing another confirmation that they truly were the new leader.

They followed up by pointing at one of the tubes and then at another gap between the white pillars further down their home. The quartet of spiders looked at their leader for a second before lighting up and running up to the mega-web.

A few moments later, they were already partway to the ground with a wide tube of webbing trailing them.

Success!

With their newfound confidence, Click activated their Skill once more and directed it at another small group of spiders.

Climb up to the web mega-structure.

Position yourselves an equal distance away from each other, covering the entire length of the web.

If you see a predator, shake the web as hard as you can.

They quickly acknowledged the command and climbed up to the top of the structure. Click saw them begin to arrange themselves and was satisfied, then looked back down to the assembled spiders before them.

The next part of the plan would be tricky. The tribe now had scouts to warn of impending danger, but now they needed someone to listen to the scouts. Spiders didn't exactly have a way of making noise like the predators and their howls, so they had to use what they had.

[Observation].

Click had to use the Skill several times on the spiders to find a few that fit what they were looking for.

> **Level 8: Web Sense**
> *Feel vibrations through created webs, even when not on them.*

Nope, not high enough. [Observation].

> **Level 7: Web Sense**
> *Feel vibrations through created webs, even when not on them.*

Nada.

> Skill level up! Observation (3)

[Observation].
[Observation].
[Observation].

> Skill level up! Observation (4)

This is taking a while.

> . . .
> Skill level up! Observation (5)

> **Level 12: Web Sense**
> *Feel vibrations through created webs, even when not on them.*
> *Identify the source of the vibrations.*

Bingo! That perk is exactly what I was looking for. [Command Subordinates]!

Skill level up! Command Subordinates (17)

Stay within the confines of the white pillars.

The lookouts above: if you feel a large vibration caused by a member of this tribe, begin to shake in warning.

Click wasn't done yet, however. They looked at another spider and sent another order.

Stay within the confines of the white pillars and web mega-structure.

Bring food to the stationary web spiders during mealtimes.

That would take care of the tribe's alarm. It wouldn't do to have the alarm system fail a few days in, after all. But what about the other spiders? What was their instinct when they saw the fear shiver in their own home?

The [Spider Commander] steeled themself and began to call [Command Subordinates] rapid-fire, bringing all of the spiders of the tribe under their control and imparting only a single quick instruction.

If you feel the fear shiver when you are already in a safe location, do not flee.

Click didn't know how well the Skill would override an existing instinct, but it was the best they could do in the circumstances. The fear shiver would only be helpful to spiders just outside of their home. Getting everyone to flee during an attack would reduce casualties, after all, but only if they were fleeing *to* safety instead of *away* from it.

Reducing deaths wasn't enough. It made for a good start with the resources and personnel Click had, but nobody in their right mind would be satisfied by just that. Click wouldn't be truly happy until the spiders could wander the entire cave without risk of getting eaten.

The [Spider Commander] looked towards the gathered hunter spiders and raised their mandibles. There were plenty more levels to gain, after all. Click would make sure they reached them as efficiently as possible.

CHAPTER FOURTEEN

A "Fun" Hunting Trip

Do you know what keeps the Shostran Army running so smoothly? Of course, the answer is logistics, but here's another question: what is the purpose of logistics? To keep soldiers fed, clothed, armed, and otherwise content.

A soldier marches on their stomach.

You can't hold a spear or perform any fancy tricks when your fingers are frozen solid.

A happy soldier is an effective soldier.

I could go on with more of the stereotypical army platitudes, but the point stands. Content soldiers are more effective than malcontent ones, and they don't cause problems for their officers.

That is the open secret behind the effectiveness of our army. Don't worry. Neither of us will be executed for espionage if you publish that. You'd think it'd be more well known.

The Johovians down south sure didn't know it. When we fought them ten years ago, their army was practically falling apart at the seams when they reached our borders! They were forced to eat half-rotten gruel, I later came to find out. Not to mention that they had a holy day during their march and weren't allowed to observe it.

As a result, all of our skirmishes between Sys-equal groups—that is to say, both sides had the same number of soldiers with roughly matching Classes, levels, and equipment—resulted in a win for us just about every time! You never see that in other wars!

So, what I'm saying is that by taking care of your soldiers, they'll take care of your enemies.

—Excerpt from an interview with Magnus Silvershell, retired general of the Shostran Army

A home with a security alarm was only secure if whoever answered could do something about it. A state-of-the-art system that made use of several scouts, which could relay an alarm to a high-level web spider? That was good. But only having a gang of [Juvenile Dungeon Hunter Spiders] answering the call? Not so much. Which was why it was time for Click to raise an army.

The [Spider Commander] looked at their soldiers. They were eager, but young and weak from inexperience. To be fair, Click was just as old as they were but had much more experience. After all, the lead spider knew how to get it.

[Command Subordinates]. Click led a band of web spiders over to a rocky outcropping near their white-pillared home. The hunter spiders followed along eagerly, but something about their mannerisms changed when their leader began to order the web spiders to begin netting up the area.

The hunters outright froze when they received their next order.

Form a line.

One at a time, climb onto the closest web.

Place webbing on it.

Move to the next web.

Repeat the previous two steps until you reach the last web.

Climb off the last web and return here.

Click looked at their army with a hint of confusion. For a few seconds after the Skill activated, the faces of the hunters displayed utter bafflement.

Click.

The show of frustration snapped the spiders out of whatever fugue had caught them, and they scurried to their task.

It was a slow process as most of the hunters had never used [Silk Spinning] before. Some of them took to it better than their brethren, but that only caused more problems as the speedier spiders would constantly be bumping into whoever was next in line, and the slower members would hold things up and create massive gaps in the queue.

Another application of [Command Subordinates] split the remaining spiders into three lines instead of one to help alleviate the worst of the delays but didn't do anything about the core problem. But it didn't matter; soon enough, the hunters were finished adding to the massive web. They even began to jitter afterwards! It was likely out of happiness, Click figured. Or relief.

But the [Spider Commander] was beginning to feel that their subordinates would soon get restless. They were hunters; they needed to hunt! And that was exactly what they would do next.

The spiders stood to attention as Click took their place at the front and directed the hunting party out into the cave. Their previous enthusiasm returned when they made contact with a small swarm of flying insects. The hunter spiders readied themselves to pounce, fangs bared and eyes sharp.

Before they could jump at the flies, the [Spider Commander] directed them to walk *around* the swarm while keeping their eyes locked on it. Once more, they wavered for a few moments before committing to the instructions and following Click's lead. Venom dripped from the hunting party's fangs as they stared unblinkingly at their would-be prey, kept away from their prizes by their leader's instruction. Order or not, they had faith they would get it in the end.

When they were finally on the other side, the [Spider Commander] finally released the hunters. The spiders ran, jumped, and otherwise swarmed the insects. The first few waves of hunters caught many of the flies and began to consume their spoils but their meal was interrupted.

Keep chasing the swarm forward!

They did as they were told, pushing the swarm back the way they had come. Some of them still had bugs dangling from their mouths as they ran and even tried getting a few chews in between jumps.

Eventually, they reached the webbing they had contributed to, and the swarm flew right into the sticky silk.

The hunter spiders looked on as their quarry suddenly stopped in place. They didn't know what to do; something like that had never happened before. It took a minute of Click pointing at the webbing and running into it themself before the others finally understood: this was what webs were for!

The hunting party lethargically approached the web, their excitement from chasing the flies as dried up as the insects would be after the spiders had had their fill.

Click regarded the group with even more confusion. Food always made spiders happy; what was going on? The [Spider Commander] figured it might have been that there wasn't enough food to satisfy everyone. They had the hunter spiders follow along for another expedition.

Another swarm of flies fell as efficiently as the first, and a third was trapped and consumed just as fast.

Skill level up! Command Subordinates (17)

Click was proud of how they'd streamlined Experience gain through their discovery of Experience sharing from cooperative webs. The bugs that gave out five points each would normally provide all of their Experience if only one spider had caught and killed them. However, when the prey was caught in a web woven by multiple spiders, each of those spiders would get three Experience points. And it didn't matter how many spiders contributed to the web; they would *all* gain three points each.

It was what let Click evolve out of their juvenile form so quickly compared to the others, and it was what was letting several members of the hunting party evolve right now.

No white glow or magical symbolism surrounded the spiders blessed with a transformation. They simply began to grow and change shape, morphing into their non-juvenile forms. Most of them became the next stage of hunter spiders, according to Click's [Observation] Skill. A few others who happened to take well to spinning webs became [Ambush Spiders].

The [Spider Commander] was ready to celebrate this explosive growth but had to put that idea on hold: some of the newly evolved spiders had begun to kick and shove their smaller brethren. Of course, their tinier counterparts fought back, and neither side seemed to be pulling their punches, judging by the spider blood that began to drip from everyone's forming wounds.

What are you doing?! Click screamed internally. *[Command Subordinates]!*

Skill level up! Command Subordinates (19)

The spiders settled down under the influence of the Skill. That didn't last long. Mere moments after its effect lifted, the members of the hunting party began to fight each other once more. But this time, it was the smaller spiders starting things.

Click.

Of course, the sound went ignored by the others, but simply making it let Click clear their head. In that moment, the lead spider realized that [Command Subordinates] couldn't override instinct completely, but it could override it for as long as it was active.

But what instinct is causing them to lash out at each other like this?

One juvenile hunter leapt onto the larger one like it did with the predators. An evolved ambush trapper shot a wad of webbing at a smaller spider from behind, taking the tiny target by surprise and sending it flying.

Wait, that's it! It all made sense now. It was their hunting instinct! These were hunter spiders, and their true nature yearned for violence. Click's excursions had been to chase bugs, but not kill them. Their meals were served up to them on a silk platter, depriving them of the true thrill of the hunt!

A very recent memory came to the [Spider Commander] of the satisfaction they had felt when joining the [Alpha Hunter]'s party to assassinate it. Click had the same exact instinct and had already satisfied it.

The lead spider's mandibles drooped as they accepted their own hypocrisy. There was only one way to fix things.

[Command Subordinates]!

The hunter spiders looked at Click, but with frowns and lethargy.

Sorry for this sad excuse of an activity. I'm going to take you on a real *hunting trip now!*

Click let go of their control, and the spiders immediately began to cheer, arms raised in the air and mandibles formed into smiles.

That was before a loud creak echoed out from the far reaches of the cave. Every single spider looked at it and, without even thinking, began to rush towards it.

A new instinct gripped the entire spider tribe, from the hunters here to the ones back in their white-pillared home, and not a single one was immune to it. Not even Click.

They all charged towards the sound, and they didn't even know why.

CHAPTER FIFTEEN

Dungeon Raid

Go.

It wasn't an instruction Click had given, but all of the spiders followed it with just as much loyalty as they would show for one given through [Command Subordinates]. No natural hunter of the tribe was immune to it. Not even Click.

The spiders all rushed towards the source of the loud noise, following a vertical sliver of light coming from that direction. Nothing other than raw desire filled their minds; they were slaves to their instincts.

Other creatures joined them on the way. A weird species of sturdy-looking insect was first, their stubby legs doing well to carry them despite the weight of the thick, chitinous shells on their backs. Click had seen them around but had never bothered trying to eat them, as they were more armor than actual meat. With how small and slow they were, it was better to chase a fly than to herd a group of these creatures into a web.

But curiosity got the better of Click at that moment and they used [Observation].

System Query: Observation
Listing Results (1/1): Advanced Overview

Juvenile Armored Beetle (Level 4)	
Soul Link	Rockfort Hamlet Dungeon Core [????????]
Classes	N/A

Evolution Prerequisites	
Species	Baby Armored Beetle

Attributes	
Health	5
Body	3
Intellect	1
Soul	1

Level 4: Deflection
Angle equipped armor to deflect an incoming attack.

Level 9: Running Charge
Increase speed when moving in a straight, unobstructed line.

Apparently, the beetles had the System as well. Not every creature Click used the [Observation] Skill on did, which was evidenced by whether such a pop-up would appear. It was mostly the smaller and weaker creatures that didn't have that strange power. The fact that these useless beetles did came as a surprise.

After several more minutes of running, the [Spider Commander] came upon the next species: a strange flying insect. No, those weren't insects. There wasn't a single bit of chitin on them. Their wings were made of stretched leather, and they were covered in fur, similar to the predators. And just like the predators, these creatures were much larger than the spiders and could have easily fit one of the spiders into their mouths.

Click couldn't see them very well. The winged creatures were swooping down from high up in the cave, where no bioluminescent mushrooms grew, and were thus shrouded in total mystery. Click hoped that the mystery wouldn't last for much longer.

[Observation]!

System Query: Observation
Listing Results (1/1): Advanced Overview

Juvenile Dungeon Bat (Level 7)	
Soul Link	Rockfort Hamlet Dungeon Core [????????]
Classes	N/A

Evolution Prerequisites	
Species	Baby Dungeon Bat

Attributes	
Health	17
Body	10
Intellect	14
Soul	8

Level 11: Echolocation
Map out surroundings using sound. Can make out fine details and textures.

Level 7: Sonic Screech
Stun weak creatures or distract larger ones with a powerful sound.

Level 2: Farming
Assists in growing food.

Wait, growing food? Click was confused. All of the food the spiders ate was hunted, never "grown." Though if the spiders themselves were capable of growing bigger, then smaller prey insects should be able to as well. It made sense. It sounded like a good idea to try in the future, if Click's brethren didn't just eat their prey at the first chance they got.

The bat immediately swooped down close to the ground and stuck its fangs into a nearby mushroom with a thud.

Click figured it had gotten distracted by the source of light and flew into it without realizing that it was a solid, if soft, object.

The winged creature pulled its face out of the mushroom with a chunk of fungus between its teeth and began to chew.

The [Spider Commander] slowed down enough to keep looking at it and lowered their mandibles as the bat kept chewing and eventually swallowed.

The mushrooms are edible?! Instinct never directed Click or their brethren to consume the glowing fungus and instead pointed them to make a meal out of all of the tiny wriggling insects that made their home in the sprawling cave.

For a moment, curiosity gripped Click more tightly than their latest instinct, and the spider slightly diverted their path to jump and take a chunk out of a nearby mushroom. They began to chew it while continuing forward at a more sedate pace, trying to focus on its flavor rather than the gripping need to keep moving.

They made it to three chews before spitting the thing out. Out of the five or so things Click had ever eaten in their life, that mushroom was by far the worst of them! Click didn't need variety in their diet to have a refined palette, thank you very much.

Curiosity sated, the [Spider Commander] continued in the same bull rush as the others. But that didn't last long.

The third species finally showed themselves, running alongside each other in a manic sprint Click had never seen from them before. But Click had seen *them* before. Predators.

The overpowering instinct to run with the others that Click felt was challenged for a second time by a rival instinct: the desire to live. And the internal desire for survival utterly overrode the external call to run.

Click snapped out of whatever spell they were under and stopped in their tracks before jumping behind a rock for cover.

None of the predators noticed the spider, or at least none that cared.

The [Spider Commander] peeked over the barrier and saw many members of their tribe running alongside the enemy, and yet none of them were being squashed beneath the creatures' feet or scooped up into their mouths. Click didn't give it a second thought and immediately called upon their Skill.

[Command Subordinates]! [Command Subordinates]! [Command Subordinates]! Get out of there!

> Skill level up! Command Subordinates (19)

The fifty or so spiders closest to the predators were immediately gripped by Click's authority and jumped out of their original path, dodging beetles and swooping bats as they made their way behind anything that would conceal them.

The predators and other creatures continued forward undeterred, most of them not even giving notice to the erratic arthropods.

Click took a deep breath and tried to relax, taking solace in how the predators had continued to ignore them. It gave the [Spider Commander] a chance to properly consider what had happened. A powerful instinct had gripped Click and the other spiders and had made them run towards the loud noise with utter abandon, likely along with every other combat-oriented creature in the cave. Including the predators, who were uncharacteristically ignoring the other spiders as the spiders were ignoring them.

The [Spider Commander] merely had to remember what the furred creatures did to the tribe to snap out of the strange pull and flee, but something kept the others from remembering. Click frowned. The other spiders were creatures of pure instinct, and a strong enough influence would apparently override any others.

Just then, the pull from [Command Subordinates] began to fade, and as it did, the spiders under its control began to charge towards the noise once more.

What? There was still plenty of time left! Click screamed internally as the others quickly caught up to the predators. The [Spider Commander] charged just behind them, ever cognizant of any threats while doing so. Something was terribly wrong, and Click was going to get to the bottom of things.

The traveling congregation eventually arrived at the source of the sound. Click climbed on top of a stalagmite some distance away from it and looked on with trepidation. This was a part of the cave the spider had never explored before. It was on the opposite the spiders' white-pillared home, and not even the [Alpha Hunter] in all of its cocky bravery ever looked for trouble out here.

A giant slab of silvery-gray material stood tall, taller than any boulder or rocky structure in the entire cave, and perfectly covered an opening. Well, it *almost* covered all of it. The slab was cracked open just a bit, allowing just a sliver of light to shine through. It illuminated the cave far more brightly than any bioluminescent mushroom had, to the point of hurting the eyes of many of the creatures, making them take a step back.

But they didn't need to fully adjust to the light, as the slab began to move and covered the gap. It let out a terribly loud noise as it moved— the same one that had gotten everyone's attention in the first place. Once it ended, there was only one sound left.

"*Squeak!*" A creature covered in fur and less than a quarter of the size of the predators jerked its head around the cave, trying to take in all of the monsters that had come to greet it.

This is what we were all called here for? This . . . What even is it? [Observation].

Squirrel

The lone cell appeared in Click's vision. It felt weird to look at it, all of that fancy bordering for such a mundane sounding name. But with everything going on, paranoia was rich in Click's mind. Too many strange things were happening, and this was one of them. This wasn't something that could be so easily dismissed.

> Dungeon Raid! Kill the intruder!

The notification flashed past Click's eyes, and from the looks of it, they weren't the only one. Every single monster gathered reacted to the flashing words.

They all took the notification as gospel, glaring at the intruder and baring their fangs—or flat incisors, in the case of the Juvenile Armored Beetles. The squirrel didn't think twice before turning around, and that was when everyone struck.

The predators jumped, the bats swooped, and the beetles charged. And the spiders . . .

[Command Subordinates]! Click began to scream to themself over and over again.

Strike last!

> Skill level up! Command Subordinates (20)
> Skill Perk unlocked for Command Subordinates!

That was the only instruction the [Spider Commander] had time to hand out before moving on to to the next batch of their brethren. *Stop* would have also been quick, but by telling the others how to fight, they were at least more likely to follow it even after the active effect wore off. And if this squirrel was a true danger, then the other spiders would have a chance to get away rather than die with the others.

The monsters of the cave landed on the intruder in a flurry of fangs and claws while almost every single spider stayed in the back. Those that did join in were quickly torn to shreds in the ensuing fight.

By the other monsters.

The squirrel was too. Its death must have been instantaneous. The monsters realized that they'd already won the fight and jumped out of the brawl, but something shifted in the air. The creatures stared at each other, first with confusion, and then with anger.

And finally, a sudden and terrible realization hit Click. These were all natural enemies, predators and prey, and they were all gathered together for the first time.

Click readied their Skills again in an attempt to save their tribe. Unlike before, the spider could now tell that [Command Subordinates] had a decent amount of charge left, despite its repeated usage on all of the hunter spiders. Click figured it was the Skill Perk they had just earned.

The [Spider Commander]'s mind continued to wander ever so slightly, but only as a sort of coping mechanism for the immense stress. They considered theories as to why they had so much charge left in their Skill. The first theory was that it was because of how simple Click's instruction had been, and the other theory was that it was because of how little their recent command had actually influenced the others; the spiders were already going to attack—Click had just made them do it a little later.

The lead spider readied themself to use every last drop of charge [Command Subordinates] had left, but it turned out that they didn't actually have to do a thing.

Dungeon Raid repelled! Assigning rewards . . .

Participation: +50 Experience

Leadership: +100 Experience

Skill Usage Contribution: +25 Experience

. . .

Level up!

Click felt dazed as the notifications flew past their vision. Trying to follow along left them exhausted, and apparently, they weren't the only one. The other creatures of the dungeon began to reel back. Rather than trying to take out any confusion or frustration on the prey present before them, the monsters all turned around and began to head back to their homes.

Even the [Spider Commander] felt the same urge and began to lead their troops to their white-pillared haven. On the way, Click used

[Observation] on some of the other spiders and couldn't help but open their mandibles in a smile at the gains they'd made. The spiders had all gone up at least a level—especially the ones who'd actually jumped into combat with the others. Those had gone up several levels! And best of all, none of the spiders looked agitated like they had before. Even the ones who hadn't gotten in on the action were feeling relaxed.

Whatever this "Dungeon Raid" had been, it didn't look like it was as bad as Click's instincts had made it out to be. If anything, it was an easy source of Experience and enjoyment for everyone. If the intruders they faced were just like that squirrel, then the tribe would become unstoppable in no time! For once in Click's life, things were looking good.

From the Office of His Royal Majesty, Sovereign of the Shostran Kingdom:

To the fair citizens of the Rockfort Hamlet:

We are writing to inform you of the possible activation of a dungeon located near your settlement. The mage's consortium has detected an increase in magical activity within your region, and they believe the dungeon to be its source.

It is still in the early stages of activation, akin to a bear just waking from its winter slumber. The dungeon poses little active danger to the hamlet, but that is not to say it is entirely benign.

We advise all residents and livestock to keep away from the dungeon's entrance, the location of which should be marked in your town records. While the monsters within the dungeon may not be able to wander out and attack, the door is very likely to be open, and anyone unarmed would most likely perish once inside.

To prevent the dungeon from waking any further and becoming a greater danger, several teams of adventurers have been deployed on behalf of the Adventurer's Guild and have been instructed to delve into its depths in order to damage and drain it of resources. We advise you not to pay them for this service, as they will be compensated for any expenses directly from the kingdom's coffers.

Expect their arrival within a fortnight, and in the meantime, please prepare to host two to threescore able-bodied men and women.

CHAPTER SIXTEEN

Anticipation and Preparations

A great divide exists between urban and rural living. The great creature comforts offered by those in the more well-developed regions of the Shostran Kingdom stand in stark contrast to the humble livings of the frontier, which makes it quite a shame that adventurers are so quick to dismiss their more rural countrymen.

The very nature of the frontier brings about hardships and opportunities for growth that allow its residents to push their limits to unprecedented degrees, which paves the way for extreme specializations. Difficulty brings challenge, which in turn brings levels. Thus, in a land of many difficulties, one can expect incredibly high levels.

The village of Tundra's Pass, located far to the north, is forced to deal with harsh cold and a lack of good soil. The challenge to keep everyone fed under these terrible conditions has allowed its farmers to level by an unprecedented degree. Their Skills allow them to grow food so nutrient dense and filling that a single slice of their bread will beat out an entire pound of pemmican in both satiation and nutrition! For

adventurers, these make the best lightweight rations imagin-
able, and for an incredibly low cost.

So do not hesitate to visit rural communities, as the goods
they produce are likely to beat out even the most expensive
equivalents found in big cities. What each village has to offer
can be a mystery, but one that is always worth uncovering.

**—Excerpt from an angrily crumpled up and aban-
doned flier on the outskirts of Rockfort Hamlet**

"Oh dear, oh dear, oh dear," mumbled Karl Erasmus as he paced around his office. A letter sat on his worn wooden desk, every other piece of clutter around it having been cleared to give it the respect it commanded.

As Burgermeister of the Rockfort Hamlet, Karl was responsible for handling the thing. The missive from the capital was nothing but bad news. The local dungeon had awakened, and even worse, there was an army of adventurers headed to their town.

Sixty able-bodied men and women were on their way to his humble village, and they were expected to arrive any minute. The town had done all it could with the time they had been given, but it likely wouldn't be enough. There wasn't enough room to house so many people. Even if you counted the empty rooms at the tavern, the hay-matted floor of the stables, and every empty floor and unused blanket in the village's houses, there still wouldn't be enough space to accommodate all of those adventurers!

Not to mention their diets. The farmers of the hamlet worked their bodies hard and ate well to fuel themselves, but their appetites were nothing compared to fabled adventurers. Classes, higher levels, and all sorts of magical prowess boosted peoples' appetites sky-high. They would make even the most gluttonous local look like a child with food poisoning by comparison.

Karl let out a sigh. The System could be a curse in that regard, but it could also be a boon. The [Farmers] of the hamlet had their own levels in the aptly named Class and were perfectly capable of growing enough food to sate their appetites. That was the only thing Rockfort would be able to provide the adventurers.

"The kingdom's blasted bureaucrats don't give me any respect!" the burgermeister grumbled. "Couldn't even bother to spring for a proper personal courier. They had to send their missive through the regular mail."

Karl walked over to the letter, picked it up again, and scowled at the date it had been penned. Exactly two weeks ago. And exactly one and a half weeks before it had arrived. "How do they expect me to get things ready for so many people in half a week?"

The room seemed to grow red around him. Either Karl Erasmus found himself awakening as some sort of fire [Mage] in his sixties, or he was just getting too worked up. Either way, he realized it would be better to go outside than to stay in his office. Otherwise, something was going to break.

The burgermeister opened the door and walked towards the building's exit, past a similarly aged woman sitting at a desk.

"Will you be out, then, sir?" she asked.

"Yes, de—I mean, assistant. I shall be back in fifteen minutes or so."

"Very well, then, sir. I'll let anyone who stops by know that you're out."

Karl simply nodded and walked out without looking back at her.

The burgermeister didn't need an assistant. The hamlet was small enough that he knew everyone by name, and they could simply approach him for anything they wanted. Still, his wife had demanded he get himself an assistant after her last trip to the capital, where she saw how their more important bureaucrats operated.

And since everybody else in the hamlet had much better things to do than fill an utterly useless role, Karl's wife had taken the job. At least, whenever she had free time. Still, for a hobby, it was much better than what the kids were into: wandering the forest and hunting bears, gods forbid. Karl hoped that the poster they'd put up on the town bulletin would be enough to dissuade anyone from taking any unnecessary risks.

The burgermeister lost himself in his thoughts and soon lost himself on the outskirts of the hamlet. However, he remained unbothered. These woods were his back yard, after all, both figuratively *and* literally. He'd just need to turn around and—

"Hello there!"

Karl turned around to see a young man waving at him. He was dressed in chainmail armor, which strained against the bulk of his muscles, and a well-fitting steel helmet, which barely concealed his curly brown hair. His sheathed sword sat snugly in a leather scabbard hanging from his side. He was flanked by another man and a woman.

The other man was stick-thin and dressed from head to toe in studded leather. His face was partially concealed by shadows despite the sun facing the opposite direction—his mere presence almost made you want to forget about him.

The woman had black hair and piercing icy-blue eyes. She was dressed in loose brownish-gray robes that settled on her body to reveal padded armor just underneath. Her belt held different vials of multicolored liquid as well as several scrolls. Her eyes looked bored, yet they darted around the surroundings and took everything in, including Karl.

"You must be the adventurers, no?" the burgermeister replied. "We have been expecting you. Welcome to our humble hamlet. I do very much hope you will all find Rockfort to be welcoming." He concluded with a light bow.

"Wow, if I'd known Mr. Erasmus would be treating us like this, I would've become an adventurer even sooner!" The brown-haired man let out a guffaw and nudged the other two with his elbows.

They couldn't help but join in and laugh alongside him.

"How much research you three must have done to recognize me as the burgermeister! And to know my name! I am honored."

"No, Mr. Erasmus, it's us," the woman spoke this time, her cheeks beginning to flush.

The leather-clad man next to her might have had a similar reaction, but he turned his head before the burgermeister could get a better look.

"Hold on," Karl narrowed his eyes and gave the trio a good hard look. "I recognize those voices . . . I can't believe it! It really is you!"

All four ran at each other and collided in a massive hug. They stood there for several seconds before letting go, a wide smile on each of their faces.

"Something is wrong with my memory," said the burgermeister, shaking his head. "It's only been one year since you left to become adventurers and I've already forgotten about you! I watched you all grow up. What kind of a burgermeister am I? Thamus, Quintus, Cassia, and . . ."

"Just us," the armored man, Thamus, replied. He gave the older man a flat smile. They all did.

"Right, so what brings you three back here? Did you get sick of adventuring and want to come home? I wouldn't blame you if you did."

The three laughed again. Quintus, the shadowy-faced one, spoke up. "We're actually part of the adventuring group that's coming from the capital, and we just had to jump at the opportunity to visit home. So maybe we *are* a little bit homesick?"

"Well, there's nothing wrong with that!" Karl gave the three a wide smile. "But there must've been quite a bit of competition to get that spot, I reckon?"

The trio looked at each other awkwardly.

"Well . . . ," Cassia, the robed woman, began, "this job is actually supposed to be punishment detail, so there wasn't exactly much competition."

Karl's smile began to falter.

Cassia quickly caught herself and raised her hands to comfort him. "Wait, wait. We weren't punished or anything! We really did volunteer for this job because we wanted to visit back home! Honest!"

They all gave the burgermeister their best sheepish grins. Eventually, he returned one of his own. "I believe you. I know you wouldn't lie to me like that!" He took a second to collect his thoughts, and his mouth fell into a frown. "But if this really *is* a punishment, then might the other adventurers try and start trouble?"

"As if they'd start trouble with us around!" Thamus let out another guffaw as he unsheathed his sword and held it in the air. Quintus did the same with a dagger that he pointed to the side, and Cassia followed suit with a glowing red orb that appeared in her hand.

Karl burst into laughter. "I remember when you all made that pose when you were kids! To think, you've come so far that you can do it with real swords and spells now!"

The trio slowly let their arms fall while doing their best to hide the red that was spreading on their faces.

"But, really," said Cassia. "The Adventurer's Guild sent someone else who can keep everyone under control all by himself. He's the leader for the dungeon raid."

"Hmm. Well, I believe you! But it might not be easy to keep everyone under control if there isn't enough space to house them. I counted, and the half a week we got wasn't enough time to build any more housing."

"Don't worry about that," replied Thamus. "I told the group about how large Rockfort is, so they all brought tents. A few of them even have portable housing."

"They also have plenty of rations," added Quintus. "But with how bland they taste, I wouldn't be surprised if *that's* what they make a stink over."

"In that case, there's nothing to worry about!" exclaimed the burgermeister. "Our farmers have been working their butts off in the fields since the letter arrived, and there should be plenty of food for everyone within a few days."

"Speaking of food," said Thamus. "Is Renard still running the tavern? I haven't had his roast in ages."

"Of course! He's planning on making enough for the adventurers, but it'll take a while to butcher and prepare that much meat. It should be ready once you've all cleared the dungeon. Now, I'll head back into town to tell everyone that you've all arrived. Maybe you want to say 'hi' to a few old faces before you regroup with the others?"

"Yeah, that'd be good," said Quintus.

The trio slowly looked at each other with somber eyes and nodded before returning a smile. It looked a little more bittersweet than before.

CHAPTER SEVENTEEN

"This Raid Can't Possibly Go Wrong!"

The mechanics by which dungeon raids operate are still quite a mystery, but through careful observation of their behavior, we can come to many insightful conclusions.

It starts with the dungeon entering its active state. Each dungeon follows a sort of cycle, wherein it switches between active and inactive. When inactive, the entry door stays shut, and not even the greatest force of strength or magic can open it. When active, the door simply acts as any other unlocked door. Entrance and egress from the dungeon proper are trivial.

During these active states, the dungeon itself welcomes intruders using promises of treasure and combat experience to lure in adventurers and those that seek their fortunes. And despite the fact the dungeon is somehow powerful enough to maintain a sheer, inviolable barrier, people still enter, looking for a fight. Why? The answer is simple: habit. Dungeons have always been fair, always following the same overall pattern in their structure and offering the same sort of rewards.

Beyond the activity of the dungeon itself, interesting behavior can be seen from the monsters that dwell within.

The dungeon is an ecosystem, with System-blessed monsters living alongside weaker creatures, usually in a predator–prey relationship. That is not to say that only weaker creatures are prey; some monsters happen to be prey as well. Monsters fight and eat each other, growing stronger and evolving as their weaker members perish.

Much of this activity is theorized to happen during the Dungeon's inactive period, permitting the monsters to increase in population and strength in relative safety, all in order to pose a proper threat to adventurers in the future.

The biggest conclusion that can be reached from this information is that dungeons are attuned to cycles of nature as any other living being is. As plants shed their leaves and bears enter hibernation during the winter, so, too, do dungeons have their inactive period, conserving their strength for brighter times. And as plants bear fruit to tempt all manner of creatures, so, too, do dungeons open their doors and tempt adventurers with treasure.

However, the treasure is a poisoned promise and always brings death to the dungeon, either to its inhabitants or the adventurers reaching for it. Perhaps the dungeon itself is a living creature that feeds on blood and this just happens to be the best way to achieve it?

**—Estran Leabrar, discredited scholar
of the Shostran Royal Palace**

[Command Subordinates]! Hold your position!

Click and the many monsters of the cave faced down the latest of the many intruders they had been pitted against these past two weeks. Just about every single intruder tended to be small and, not surprisingly, incredibly weak. There happened to be a few more sizable ones, but they had fallen just as quickly as that first squirrel.

The [Spider Commander] did find one similarity between them, however, and that was that none of them registered with the System. Levels, Skills, attributes; all of them were missing. The only other creatures with such a lack of mystic ability in the cavern were the smallest of worms and flies the spider tribe hunted. It was a universal marker of weakness.

Or so everyone thought.

[Observation]!

Bear

That was the information the System supplied. No System, no problem, right? So why was that thing over twice the size of the largest dungeon hound?

[Observation]!

System Query: Observation Listing Results (1/1): Advanced Overview

Alpha Dungeon Hound (Level 15)	
Soul Link	Rockfort Hamlet Dungeon Core [????????]
Classes	N/A

Evolution Prerequisites	
Species	Dungeon Hound
Skill: Pack Tactics	> Level 15

Attributes	
Health	190
Body	77
Intellect	28
Soul	42

Level 15: Iron Fangs *Teeth are reinforced to be harder and sharper. Bites do not heal as easily.*

> **Level 27: Pack Tactics**
> *Instinctively understand the desires of the rest of the pack and share complex information with them. See through the eyes of pack members.*

> **Level 17: Prey Detection**
> *Instinctually sense the location of prey and its movements. Understand what the target prey is feeling.*

> **Level 7: Observation**
> *Obtain System information about a target.*

The [Alpha Hound] looked at the so-called bear with a relaxed posture, but its eyes were sharp.

But as Click looked into those red orbs, the spider could see that it wasn't because of any kind of fear or concern about the unknown creature. The predator was simply looking through System menus. With its high-leveled Skills and its numerous additional perks, the hound was probably overwhelmed with information, and it all likely said the same thing.

[Observation] would've returned no System information. [Prey Detection] likely returned the obvious: that the bear was feeling sleepy. The intruder let out a yawn, despite the careful look it gave all of the gathered monsters.

Despite being fed all sorts of obvious facts by the System, the [Alpha Hound] was seemingly missing one crucial detail: the bear was bigger than anything else. Underneath that fur, muscles rippled as the beast stretched.

And the leader hound relaxed its gaze.

Click flexed their mandibles in the spider equivalent of a scoff. The moniker of "alpha" really suited the predators' leader; it was just as stupid as the [Alpha Hunter] had been. Especially because it sent its own packmates to attack the bear first.

All drowsiness left the eyes of the beast in an instant, and it raised its front left paw to attack. A single swipe sent three predators flying back.

When they landed, they all struggled to get back up. A large red puddle was beginning to form beneath the group, and terrible cracking sounds could be heard as they rose to their feet.

The [Alpha Hound] panicked, but rather than brashly throwing more warm bodies at the bear, it sent several predators to flank the beast.

Click felt a little disappointed. While the foreign and incredibly powerful instinct told them to be happy for having such strong teammates in this battle, the [Spider Commander] knew that they would be enemies again soon after. But in the meantime, better partners meant a faster fight, and that meant faster Experience before the next inevitable invasion.

As the predators took their position behind the bear, the beetles that had just arrived began their charge. The armored insects' much smaller size didn't let them do anything as crazy as toppling the intruder, but their sharpened horns forced it to jump out of the way.

That was the opening the dungeon hounds were looking for, and they took the opportunity to jump into the fray. While the bear tried to address every incoming attack with a single motion, a pair of swooping bats going for its eyes threw it even further off balance, making its strike go wide.

The hounds' [Iron Fangs] activated, and three pairs of yellow-stained teeth cleaved through flesh. The dungeon hounds began to shake their muzzles in an attempt to rend flesh, but their Skill began to wear off. While they weren't able to do anything as drastic as tearing the bear's front limb off, each of their movements was able to draw blood.

The beast roared with all its might. The sound echoed off the cavern walls and into the sensitive ears of half the species present. Bats and predators reeled back, and the ones still hooked onto the bear's front limb loosened their grip, never having heard such an ear-shattering sound before.

That was all the opportunity the bear needed, and it slammed its front paw into the ground. The hounds that were attached finally let go. But the bear wasn't done yet, and it followed up by slashing the trio's necks with its other paw. They didn't even let out a whimper after the attack—only blood.

But some of the blood beginning to pool behind the bear was its own.

The rest of the monsters saw their opportunity this time, and all charged at the bear in unison. The beast rose up on its hind legs and began to swat at the bats, stomp at the beetles, and bite at the hounds that came after it.

All the while, Click held their own troops in reserve. Watching. Waiting. Then the battle began in earnest.

[Command Subordinates]. Wait.

A dungeon hound tore at the bear's back leg.

[Command Subordinates]. Do not engage.

Several bats dropped some kind of an acidic liquid, which managed to fall right into the bear's eyes, blinding it.

[Command Subordinates]. Reposition yourselves to a rock that's closer by but stay hidden!

Several beetles rushed at the intruder's feet and pushed it onto its back.

[Command Subordinates]. Now! Charge in and bite!

A surge of spiders came flooding at the bear, running past the other monsters that were on top of it, biting and piercing its weakened body. Envenomed fangs too small to be stopped by the thick fur pierced through the supple skin and tainted the blood underneath. Every spider managed to get a bite in, and even Click somehow got a hit in, albeit from a thrown pebble.

While every creature was biting and clawing, a pair of web spiders that had been dragged along carried a web towards the downed bear and draped the small silk netting over its side. It would do nothing to the massive beast, but that wasn't what was important. The fact that it had been woven by every single web spider back home *was*.

The attacks continued, and soon enough, the beast succumbed to the onslaught and lay dead on the cavern floor. A wave of euphoria rushed through everyone present, and they quickly began to head back to their homes, ignoring the enemies now beside them. The predators, however, decided to drag the corpse of the intruder along with them, most likely to make it a meal that would feed them all for days. Nobody else objected.

> Dungeon Raid repelled! Assigning rewards . . .
> Participation: +50 Experience
> Leadership: +100 Experience
> Assistance: +500 Experience

Everything was the same as the first completed raid, except for the presence of the Assistance bonus. Apparently, merely leading troops into battle didn't count for much, and Click was given the same amount of Experience no matter what they fought, be it a harmless squirrel or this monstrous bear. Doing damage to the enemy on the other hand . . .

And all I had to do was toss a pebble at it! I must have dealt less than a single point of Damage and I still *get so much Experience!* The [Spider Commander] couldn't help but feel smug. This way they were able to get the most Experience, but that Experience wouldn't be restricted to just them and the hunter spiders; the useless web that had been thrown on the bear earlier would've counted towards the *web* spiders' Participation in the fight as well and would've granted them the same in Experience. They would need it, since they were apparently the only exception to the raid's call to action.

No matter. Click knew that the web spiders kept the actual troops fed and was grateful they could let the others concentrate on fighting and gaining Experience. A mutual trade. Food for Experience, and at a much better rate than killing flies that had landed on the webs.

The [Spider Commander] had begun to walk back home when they noticed one of their troops beginning to transform. While Click expected it to turn into a bigger version of its current self, a Dungeon Hunter Spider, it instead turned into something . . . different. It was much too big.

[Observation]. What did my spider just evolve into?

System Query: Observation
Listing Results (1/1): Advanced Overview

Dungeon Spider Bruiser (Level 1)

Soul Link	Rockfort Hamlet Dungeon Core [????????]
Classes	N/A

Evolution Prerequisites

Species	Dungeon Hunter Spider

Base	Per level	Attribute
35	7	Health
20	5	Body
5	2	Intellect
8	3	Soul

Venom Gland

Secrete a toxic substance from the mandibles that can harm lesser creatures.

Silk Spinning

Secrete a sticky string that can ensnare weaker creatures.

Prey Detection

Instinctually sense the location of prey and its movements.

Iron Carapace

Exoskeleton is reinforced to be harder and more durable.

Become Stone

Temporarily become petrified to negate non-physical damage.

A [Spider Bruiser]? It's strong! Nowhere near as powerful as the [Alpha Hunter], but I'll gladly take someone who can take a hit.

Several of the other spiders began to transform too, many of them also enlarging into the form of a bruiser. But "many" didn't mean all. Most of the other hunter spiders became larger as well but looked nothing like the bruisers. Rather, they were simply a slightly bigger version of their old selves.

[*Observation*].

System Query: Observation
Listing Results (1/1): Advanced Overview

Adult Dungeon Hunter Spider (Level 1)

Soul Link	Rockfort Hamlet Dungeon Core [????????]
Classes	N/A

Evolution Prerequisites

Species	Dungeon Hunter Spider

Base	**Per level**	**Attribute**
25	4	Health
18	4	Body
5	2	Intellect
7	3	Soul

Venom Gland
Secrete a toxic substance from the mandibles that can harm lesser creatures.

Silk Spinning
Secrete a sticky string that can ensnare weaker creatures.

Prey Detection
Instinctually sense the location of prey and its movements.

What was that?! Click couldn't help but think. *It's the exact same thing! The attributes are a little better than they were previously, but still . . . it's the same thing!*

Click felt a small pang of guilt go through them. Here they were, judging their brethren for their lackluster evolution when the change from the juvenile commander stage to the mature one was just the same.

Well, I hope things are a little juicier next time.

Click was getting ready to head back when they saw that the string of evolutions wasn't complete. The [Ambush Spiders] made up a very small minority of the arachnid forces, yet they, too, were transforming at a similar, if not greater, rate.

These spiders evolved into two different variants, each similar in their lithe builds when compared to the hunters and their evolutions, but quite different from each other in every other way.

The first variant had a light red shade over its otherwise neutral brown thorax and head. Its abdomen, however, was tinted blue and differently shaped, looking as if additional hydraulic muscles were lining the length of the structure.

[Observation].

System Query: Observation
Listing Results (1/1): Advanced Overview

Dungeon Web Slinger Spider (Level 1)	
Soul Link	Rockfort Hamlet Dungeon Core [????????]
Classes	N/A

Evolution Prerequisites	
Species	Dungeon Ambush Trapper Spider
Skill: Silk Spinning	> Level 20
Skill: Web Launch	> Level 15

Base	**Per level**	**Attribute**
20	5	Health

15	4	Body
7	4	Intellect
8	3	Soul

Venom Gland
Secrete a toxic substance from the mandibles that can harm lesser creatures.

Silk Spinning
Secrete a sticky string that can ensnare weaker creatures.

Prey Detection
Instinctually sense the location of prey and its movements.

Excretion Launcher
Eject any excreted bodily substance at high velocity.

3D Move Sense
Instinctually understand where a moving object will go in 3D space.

And so many new Skills! It looks even better at catching things in its thrown webs! But where did [Web Launch] go?

Click was curious, if not a little confused, but then reread the description for [Excretion Launcher]. [Web Launch] and [Excretion Launcher] were essentially the same thing, but the words "any excreted bodily substance" and "high velocity" set the latter apart. Perhaps it was an upgraded version of [Web Launch] and the weaker redundant Skill was removed? It would be terrible if the old Skill was strengthened to an incredibly high degree, only for all of that progress to be lost.

Thankfully, it wasn't in this case, or in any of the other cases of spiders evolving into [Web Slingers].

The other evolution Click observed was also interesting. Rather than red and blue, these spiders turned gray. And they especially hated light. They ran away from the brightest of the bioluminescent mushrooms and the sliver of light from the cracked-open door, fleeing into the shadows, where they practically dissolved in the additional darkness.

[Observation].

System Query: Observation
Listing Results (1/1): Advanced Overview

Dungeon Shadow Spider (Level 1)	
Soul Link	Rockfort Hamlet Dungeon Core [????????]
Classes	N/A

Evolution Prerequisites	
Species	Dungeon Ambush Trapper Spider
Skill: Venom Gland	> Level 20
Skill: Web Launch	> Level 10

Base	**Per level**	**Attribute**
15	4	Health
15	5	Body
8	3	Intellect
7	4	Soul

Venom Gland
Secrete a toxic substance from the mandibles that can harm lesser creatures.

Silk Spinning
Secrete a sticky string that can ensnare weaker creatures.

Prey Detection
Instinctually sense the location of prey and its movements.

<table>
<tr><td>Web Launch
Hold and throw your webbing.</td></tr>
</table>

<table>
<tr><td>Sneak
Shadows and obstacles provide better concealment from others.</td></tr>
</table>

<table>
<tr><td>Shadow Travel
Move more quickly while concealed in darkness or shadow.</td></tr>
</table>

Click was at a loss for words, and not just because they didn't know how to speak any. They weren't shocked speechless, like they had been with the [Alpha Hunter], but the [Spider Commander] was locked in serious thought.

The new Skills looked very interesting but were completely different from how a spider would normally operate. [Sneak] and [Shadow Travel] weren't quite things Click had worked with before, but the spider was able to quickly wrap their head around what this new evolution could do. Ambushes, but from the shadows, and even better than before.

Seeing that the rest of the group had finished their evolutions, Click dragged everyone back home, still awash in the post-raid euphoria. As they arrived back, Click could see some of the web spiders had also changed. The [Spider Commander] raised their mandibles in a smile as they realized their plan of making them "participate" had paid off.

Hold on, is that . . . [Observation].

<table>
<tr><td>System Query: Observation
Listing Results (1/1): Advanced Overview</td></tr>
</table>

Dungeon Web Slinger Spider (Level 1)	
Soul Link	Rockfort Hamlet Dungeon Core [????????]
Classes	N/A

Evolution Prerequisites	
Species	Adult Dungeon Web Spider
Skill: Silk Spinning	> Level 30

Base	Per level	Attribute
20	5	Health
15	4	Body
7	4	Intellect
8	3	Soul

Venom Gland
Secrete a toxic substance from the mandibles that can harm lesser creatures.

Silk Spinning
Secrete a sticky string that can ensnare weaker creatures.

Prey Detection
Instinctually sense the location of prey and its movements.

Excretion Launcher
Eject any excreted bodily substance at high velocity..

3D Move Sense
Instinctually understand where a moving object will go in 3D space.

It's the same exact evolution, but with a slightly different prerequisite! Click thought hard for a few moments before coming to a conclusion. *Perhaps the evolution branches can converge? I was given the choice to become a specialized hunter or web spider twice, after all.*

The newly minted [Web Slinger] shifted in its net and waved at the approaching group. A fly passed the spider, and it idly threw a web that caught and reeled it in. After eating it, the [Web Slinger] sat down and looked out to the cave in contentment.

It looks like evolution doesn't define a spider's instinct, then. That's still definitely a web spider, through and through!

Click was about to retire for the day and get themself a nice feast from the web when the large door at the end of the cave began to creak open again.

What, so soon?

Dungeon Raid! Kill the intruder!

The notification flashed across the [Spider Commander]'s vision, and with it came a feeling of urgency. But the euphoria from the previous raid was still swimming in their head, and the two feelings clashed. Click began to feel a little dizzy and tried to right themself with a quick meal.

Experience +3
Level up!
Level requirement achieved for evolution
Choices available: Dungeon Spider Army Commander, Dungeon Spider Mimicry Commander, Alpha Dungeon Spider Commander
Please select an option

The notifications made Click feel a little better but didn't offset the dizziness. Something was very wrong about this situation; the [Spider Commander] knew it and didn't want to make a bad choice.

Wait, let me see what's raiding us first!

Please select an option

At least let me . . . [Command Subordina—

Please select an option

The System notification interrupted the Skill.

I have a really bad feeling about this . . .

"Hey, anyone in here?" came a shout from the back of the cavern.

"Shut up, idiot! Do you want them to hear us?" replied another voice.

"Calm down. This dungeon raid is going to be a cinch!" said the first. "Besides, we *want* to get their attention!"

CHAPTER EIGHTEEN

A VERY Nervous Choice

The concept of the adventuring party was coined specifically for the exploration of dungeons. Even though these dangerous structures attract both the brave and foolhardy alike, it would not be accurate to say that these types are one and the same. The prospect of wealth and fame attracts those who know how to get things done.

Anyone entering a dungeon will bring forth its wrath, and the more people who intrude into its confines, the more forceful the response. That is why parties are recommended to be between three and five members in size. More than that would trigger an overwhelming assault while fewer would leave too much of a burden on each member.

Raw strength is not all that an adventuring party must worry about, however. The monsters within a dungeon are capable of basic tactics such as ambushes and flanking, and a party composition tailored to fighting against such guerilla threats must be carefully considered.

That's not to mention the traps that occasionally appear in dungeons as well. Pitfalls, poison gas, and, in some cases, giant falling boulders speak of powerful engineers, yet there is never any creature within a dungeon intelligent enough to have built it themself.

Never have the true masterminds behind dungeon traps shown themselves, so there is, thankfully, little reason to dwell on the idea. But oddities like these inspired the creation of the standards, which everyone follows. Keep safe and, like the minds who came up with these standards, stay sharp.

—Excerpt from *Dungeoneering: A Primer* by Almidus Goldring, dungeon scholar and one-time adventurer

"This dungeon raid's going to be a cinch! Besides, we *want* to get everyone's attention!" exclaimed an excited voice at the back of the cave.

A moment later, a loud thud echoed out from the same place.

"Hey, what was that for?!" the voice exclaimed even more loudly, sounding like it was in pain.

"Be quiet! Getting everything's attention is *their* job, not ours! We're just here to scout." This voice was higher pitched, yet its words were whispered in a low, harsh growl.

"You mean *you're* here to scout," pouted the first voice, brought down to an equally soft whisper.

Click didn't understand what those words meant, but the spider had definitely never heard anything like them before. There wasn't a discernable pattern to the sounds, like a series of barks, chirps, or clicks, which held simple meaning. The series of differing vowels and the multitude of consonants held a terrible complexity that Click didn't even know how to begin parsing. The only thing the spider was able to understand was that it gave them a very bad feeling.

And that wasn't all. The intruders had triggered the dungeon raid message that the monsters of the cavern had become all too familiar with. But the feeling of urgency that came with the notification mixed with the euphoric feeling from completing the previous raid to create an incredibly disorienting mix.

Oh yeah, and to top it all off, there was also one other annoying message.

> Level requirement achieved for evolution
> Choices available: Dungeon Spider Army Commander, Dungeon Spider Mimicry Commander, Alpha Dungeon Spider Commander
> Please select an option

The [Spider Commander] didn't *want* to make a choice! At least not before fully assessing the situation, but that hypocrite of a System wasn't letting Click have a choice themself.

Fine! Show me the choices! the spider internally screamed as they tried to make sense of the menus that appeared before them.

> Listing result (1/3): Advanced Evolution Overview

Dungeon Spider Army Commander	
Evolution Prerequisites	
Species	Dungeon Spider Commander
Intellect	> 30
Skill: Command Subordinates	> Level 20

Base	Per level	Attribute
15	3	Health
8	2	Body
15	5	Intellect
8	4	Soul

> **Venom Gland**
> *Secrete a toxic substance from the mandibles that can harm lesser creatures.*

Silk Spinning
Secrete a sticky string that can ensnare weaker creatures.

Command Subordinates
Command subordinate members of your organization. They will follow your will as if it were an instinct.

Observation
Obtain System information about a target.

One Army, One Being
Only one Skill check is used in System interactions with a designated group.

The numbers looked fine to Click; they were higher than their current evolution. More Health to not die from an attack, more Body to quickly move into position and run away. Intellect was always nice to help make smarter decisions. And Soul? Well, bigger numbers were always better when they were your own.

But the new Skill, [One Army, One Being], gave Click pause while they tried to make sense of it. The first thought that popped up in the spider's mind when they read the words "System interactions" was of outsider attacks based on Skills, such as venom. Would poisoning one of the spiders of a group poison them all?

Click stumbled while trying to think about it more but caught their balance before they hit their head against a massive pebble. The adrenaline that flowed through them at the near-injury brought them enough focus to come to an epiphany. Click's *own* Skills would only need to be cast once to affect an entire group!

[Command Subordinates] could control a few dozen of Click's brethren, but with groups of four or five spiders each, the Skill would be able to affect many times that number of spiders with a single cast! So much of its limited fuel could be saved, and Click would be able to enforce more finely tuned control over their troops.

A foreign pressure exerted itself over Click and urged them to take this evolution. It felt like an instinct, but it didn't come from the spider's mind or body. It felt a lot like the dungeon raid call.

Still, the [Spider Commander] was curious about the other choices and urged the System to display the next one.

Before the menu could pop up, a series of howls erupted from the back of the cave, followed by quickening footsteps.

"Yarric, please do not provoke the hounds. We still need to scout." This voice was also higher pitched and utterly serene but sounded slightly different. It likely belonged to another one of the intruders—someone cool and calculated, a natural, nuanced leader. Just like Click.

"What are you talking about? I'm still right behind you!" said the deeper voice. It somehow kept pitching higher and higher every time its owner spoke, as if it was distressed but at the same time incredibly bored. Something about it was reminiscent of the old [Alpha Hunter].

"We don't have to be looking directly at you to know you're going to throw that rock in your hand at them," the first, higher-pitched voice retorted. It reminded Click of a dungeon hound's bark, the kind they usually gave right before attacking. "You're only supposed to fight if they come to us, not the other way around. Besides, we've still got the rest of the floor to scout."

A small thud echoed out from the trio; it was the sound of a stone falling to the ground.

"Damn rogues. And this sneaking crap," the deeper voice mumbled. It was low and more deeply pitched again, and it rang of disappointment. Click couldn't help but give off a smile.

But the grin soon fell as footsteps from the three echoed ever closer to Click and the spider tribe.

Listing result (2/3): Advanced Evolution Overview	
Alpha Dungeon Spider Commander	
Evolution Prerequisites	
Species	Dungeon Spider Commander

Intellect	> 50
Skill: Command Subordinates	> Level 20

Base	Per level	Attribute
25	5	Health
10	4	Body
15	5	Intellect
8	4	Soul

Venom Gland

Secrete a toxic substance from the mandibles that can harm lesser creatures.

Silk Spinning

Secrete a sticky string that can ensnare weaker creatures.

Command Subordinates

Command subordinate members of your organization. They will follow your will as if it were an instinct.

Observation

Obtain System information about a target.

Pack Tactics

Instinctively understand the desires of the rest of the pack and share complex information with them.

The numbers were even bigger this time! And that Skill, [Pack Tactics]! Ever since Click had seen the [Alpha Hound] using it, the spider had wanted it for themself. And here was a perfect opportunity to finally obtain it. But one little word in the series of menus left a particularly sour taste in the [Spider Commander]'s mouth.

Alpha. The sounds that made up the word were all lost to the relatively mute spider, but the meaning remained. The top, the best, the peak. It was also the title that the [Alpha Hunter] had gone by. The idiot.

Click shivered slightly in rage, and the sudden emotion pulled them out of their haze enough to better consider the choice. Or rather, it helped the spider remember why they hated the moniker of "alpha." Associations with arrogance and stupidity made the [Spider Commander] call for the next option.

"Woah, what's that over there? Are those spider webs? They're taking up at least fifty square feet of the wall!"

"Don't make stuff up; there's no way there'll be that much webbing here. This is supposed to be a low-level dungeon! It's probably—woah."

"We ought to report this to the raid leader."

"Or maybe we should take it down so it won't get in their way? Come on, that thing is huge! Let's burn it to the ground!"

"Only you would charge into a fight against something you don't know anything about. How about we save the butt whooping until *after* we take a closer look, hmm?"

Listing result (3/3): Advanced Evolution Overview

Dungeon Spider Mimicry Commander	
Evolution Prerequisites	
Species	Dungeon Spider Commander
Intellect	> 25
Skill: Command Subordinates	> Level 20

Base	Per level	Attribute
15	3	Health
7	2	Body
12	5	Intellect
8	3	Soul

> **Venom Gland**
> *Secrete a toxic substance from the mandibles that can harm lesser creatures.*

> **Silk Spinning**
> *Secrete a sticky string that can ensnare weaker creatures.*

> **Command Subordinates**
> *Command subordinate members of your organization. They will follow your will as if it were an instinct.*

> **Observation**
> *Obtain System information about a target.*

> **Camouflage**
> *Change color to match with the surroundings.*

The numbers weren't as good overall, but [Camouflage] looked interesting. It would be a good way to hide from enemies and better command troops.

The footsteps were getting closer, and a bright orange light came with them. The source of the glow entered Click's view first as a flame from behind a rock. A stick appeared below it, which was held in the left hand of the intruder in the front. All three of the raiders looked over to the web, and despite the foreignness of their species, Click could instinctively identify the horror on their faces as they reached for their weapons.

Panic filled the [Spider Commander]'s heart as they realized they didn't have any time left to choose. There was a battle coming, and they would need power. Click gave in to the foreign instinct and made their choice.

> Evolution option selected: Dungeon Spider Army Commander
> Beginning evolution . . .

Click found it surprising that the transformation didn't take very long and even more surprising that they had ended up mostly the same except for the pattern on their thorax; it had gained an extra color—a swirl of red to accompany the jagged lines of yellow. But that wasn't what surprised Click the most. It was the fact that none of the intruders had even noticed the spider's change, or even the fact that it had happened right in front of the group.

The diminutive leader scurried back to the safety of the white pillars on flailing legs, not even bothering to properly articulate their Skill's instructions as they headed up the webbing.

[Command Subordinates]! [Command Subordinates]! [Command Subordinates]! To me!

Click mentally screamed out their Skill several more times until all two-hundred-and-something spiders were gathered within their web, gazing down at the three challengers.

"Uh, are they supposed to do that? Damn it, this was supposed to be a scouting mission, not a fight!" exclaimed one of the intruders in the back. She was swaddled in a padded chest piece and pants made of something that looked like the hairless skin of the predators, but her hands were wrapped in reflective gray gauntlets, one of which was idly scratching at her upper lip.

"Unlike you, I'm thanking the gods for giving me a fight! It was getting boring just following you two." The person next to her followed her gaze and almost jumped back when he saw the almost two thousand eyes staring back at him. His armor matched the color and sheen of the woman's gloves, but where her gloves were interlocking plates, his armor was patterned in a scale-like formation.

"I would expect dungeon spiders to try to run in and kill us, but this behavior seems . . . strange. They're simply staring at us with that static expression, likely lost in their own thoughts without a hint of understanding ours. I do wonder what they're thinking," replied the woman holding the torch. Everything she wore, even the cowl that concealed her face, was made of a similarly hairless skin-like material but dyed a shade of black that seemed to blend in with the shadows. Which was unfortunate for her, as the torch banished any shadowy hiding places nearby. "But they're watching . . . waiting for us to make a move."

Click kept all eight of their eyes on the trio, not daring to look away. They were definitely talking about something, maybe about whether to attack? But with the dizziness Click and the rest of the tribe felt, attacking now would be inopportune.

"Come on, you can't seriously believe that dungeon spiders can think?" asked the scale-armor-clad man. "Maybe it's just raid sickness that has them acting up? We should probably torch this whole thing before they jump at us."

The woman with the gauntlets seemed to snap out of whatever trance she had been in and replied, "Then what's the deal with their web? That thing has to have been made with teamwork."

"Well, whatever the answer to that conundrum is, they're not trying to pick a fight, and they'd be a pain if they did. So, the best course of action would be to keep moving."

The man pouted. "Yeah, but—"

"Our job is just to scout the first floor and yours is to guard us. We would be little use in a fight with a swarm, and we have responsibilities beyond that. Now, come along; we still have a job to do."

The shadow-clad leader walked away, and the gauntleted woman followed behind. The armored man looked between the rest of his team and the mega-web and let out a sigh before following in the others' wake.

Click felt a wave of relief wash over them, but that didn't last long once their command Skill began to slip. Using it to control every available spider took too much System energy, and now that it and the dizziness were beginning to wane, the [Spider Commander] wouldn't be able to keep their tribe under control for much longer.

If only there was a way to make using this easier . . . Wait. I'm an idiot, and I'm not even an alpha!

Stress and dizziness had made Click completely forget about their evolution and the brand-new Skill they had acquired.

Time to put it to use. [One Army, One Being]!

A group of four spiders fell under its effect. They didn't come to attention or show any outward sign of falling under the influence of the Skill, but Click knew they had become a sort of singular target.

Skill level up! One Army, One Being (2)

[One Army, One Being]! [One Army, One Being]! [One Army, One Being] . . .

Skill level up! One Army, One Being (3)

A group of five fell under its effects this time.

Skill level up! One Army, One Being (4)

Then a group of six.

Skill level up! One Army, One Being (5)

. . .

Somehow, the Skill wasn't tiring. Whatever System-ordained resource [One Army, One Being] utilized, it wasn't as costly as [Command Subordinates]. And they didn't even draw from the same pool, so when the [Spider Commander] took control of the entire tribe, it used almost a sixth of the energy as before.

Maybe this was the right evolutionary choice after all.

"Well, Yarric, it appears you will finally get your wish," said the woman with the torch. She pointed towards the [Alpha Hound] that had begun to summon its still-dizzy pack towards the intruders.

"Welp, we can't have that," replied the other woman, who pulled out a long, thin implement that shone just like her gloves. She flipped it in the air just above her hand, caught it on the shiny side, and threw it with a casual flick. The long instrument sailed through the air and embedded itself into the [Alpha Hound]. The predator didn't even let out a shriek as the blade pierced its throat. It just collapsed, and the rest of its pack chose to flee.

"Oh, come on! That was my kill!" exclaimed the armored man. "You owe me an *actual* fight with something now!"

The killer continued forward. "Calm down. You've wasted enough time so far that the monsters will probably get over their raid sickness before we finish."

Click paled as they watched the three casually move on. If they were able to instantly spot a powerful leader like that, maybe the spider *should've* become a [Mimicry Commander]?

CHAPTER NINETEEN

Very Peculiar Intruders

Dungeon disarmament is a tricky subject, and not entirely due to the difficulty; politics also play a large role in its overall implementation.

Dungeons are often referred to as an aspect of nature in that, just like the trees, they wake and sleep depending on the season, albeit following their own internal clocks. When dungeons are active, they invite adventurers to risk their lives in pursuit of untold riches beneath the earth. However, when left to grow in strength, dungeons will spill forth the monsters from within to wreak havoc on the surrounding lands.

This latter case is where dungeon disarmament comes into play. When enough damage is dealt to a dungeon—its monsters killed, structures damaged, and loot plundered—it will re-enter a state of hibernation and close its doors for an extended period of time.

And that extended period of time is where controversy arises. When delved at a sustainable rate, dungeons can nourish a local economy for years without ever entering hibernation. Adventurers require supplies, arms, and armor for their expeditions, and they are very likely to purchase them as close to their target as possible.

That means settlements located near popular dungeons have an incentive to stand against dungeon disarmament. However, that does not apply to all towns. Those located on the fringes of the kingdom stand in favor of dungeon disarmament; when the danger posed by dungeons is weighed against how few people travel so far out to explore them, there is little appreciable benefit for the town.

As it stands, the current policy for dungeon disarmament is to take input from its nearby towns to determine whether the practice should be followed. This has caused some problems in the past, however, when settlements have wished to supplement their economy without having insight into how their dungeon works. Adventurers are eventually sent forth either way, whether to protect the town or to clean up the corpses.

—Excerpt from *Political Treatise on Dungeoneering* by Almidus Goldring, dungeon scholar and one-time adventurer

Click swore to themself. Or, at least, the spider equivalent of chewing oneself out. They knew they didn't deserve that kind of criticism, even from themself, but the mistakes that hindsight revealed to them felt much too embarrassing.

[Observation]! Come on, [Observation]!

The intruders were too far away. Click would have had the perfect chance to get some information about the strange beings when they approached the mega-web, but the dizziness all the monsters were feeling prevented the [Spider Army Commander] from making use of their greatest asset: common sense.

From where they were seated, at least, Click was in position to get the next best thing.

"Charging beetles on our left," said the woman at the front of the group. She fidgeted uncomfortably under the bright light of her torch, which stood in contrast to her shadow-colored clothing.

"I got it!" exclaimed the man standing at the back. He aggressively jumped forward with a shield and sword in his hands and blocked the oncoming charge with the slab of thin gray material. He didn't even flinch when the beetles impacted.

"Finally having fun, Yarric?" teased the other woman of the group. She held a pair of throwing knives in her gauntleted right hand.

"Yeah, just sitting here with my shield up is *super* fun," Yarric deadpanned in a low growl.

"Hey, that [Alpha Hound] went down in a single hit. That wasn't fun either!"

"I bet the experience you got was, though!"

"Enough, you two," the first woman spoke with a raised voice, and despite its serene monotone, it carried enough force of will to quiet the others. "Scouting the creatures is just about done, so let's complete our last task."

Click watched as the trio turned around and headed towards a corner of the cave that none of the spiders had ever entered before. It was at an angle that couldn't easily be seen from the web, so the [Spider Army Commander] began to follow them with a contingent of hunter spiders.

The spiders' path was thankfully clear, and even if it hadn't been, the fact that the dungeon raid was active would have kept other monsters from attacking them. They set themselves up a safe distance away and began watching. This wasn't somewhere any of them had ever been before, so Click was very curious about what had gotten the intruders' attention.

The woman in the front handed the torch to the lady with the gauntlets and bent down to inspect the ground in front of a downward-facing tunnel. Her deft hands moved with considerable grace as she dug at the rough topsoil and pulled at some sort of invisible mechanism. At least, that was what it looked like. She very well could have been fumbling around for nothing, but Click wouldn't underestimate this group. Especially not after they had killed the [Alpha Hound] so quickly.

I never even knew there was another passage there. Where does it lead? Maybe there are more flies down there. Click got lost in their own thoughts.

All of a sudden, the woman jumped back as a series of sharp spikes shot out of the floor of the rocky passage. She stood still for a few seconds before slowly rising to her feet. The expression on her face looked the exact same as it had before she started.

"Nice job disarming the trap!" cheered the armored man, though Click could still make out the same frustration and disdain it always contained. "I guess it can't kill anyone else if it kills you first."

"Purposeful activation," she retorted. "Easier to do with dungeon traps, since they don't follow normal trap-building conventions. Jumping back was simply an added precaution."

"Yeah, whatever. So are we done here?"

"Yes. I'll inform the captain that they can begin." The woman placed a finger to her ear and began to speak. "Raid Leader, first floor has been scouted, and the spike trap leading to the second floor has been disarmed."

While the trio was distracted, Click and the other spiders approached them silently. Now that they were finally within range, the [Spider Army Commander] let loose their Skill.

[Observation]!

Human	
Name	Amalia Aersoul
Deity	N/A
Classes	Trapfinder Rogue

Wait, that's it? I understand what a name is; mine is Click. But what is a Class? And where are its attributes, Skills, or anything else? System, what can it do?

> Skill level up! Observation (10)
> Skill Perk unlocked for Observation!

> **Level 10: Observation**
> *Obtain System information about a target. Bypasses the target's personal desire to hide System information.*

Bypass? That implies it's possible to hide your information from others just by wanting to. Then how come I could see everyone else's info? Maybe they were just too stupid to realize all of their strengths and weaknesses were on full display in the first place?

Before the lead spider could make use of the perk, the three intruders caught Click's attention.

The woman who had disarmed the spike trap nodded to herself before looking to the other two and then to the entrance. The familiar creaking noise began to emanate from the other side of the cavern, but it was quickly replaced with a slam and the staccato of heavy footsteps.

> Dungeon Raid! Kill the intruder!
> Dungeon Raid! Kill the intruder!
> Dungeon Raid! Kill the intruder!
>
> . . .

The words flashed past Click's vision several times, and each time they did, the urge to run over to the entrance to meet the newcomers with envenomed fangs grew larger. The [Spider Army Commander] didn't even realize they were moving by the sixth message, and they had broken into a breakneck pace by the fifteenth.

By the last notification, number forty-something, the spiders had all arrived at the pale gray door, where they came to a halt. A massive shining rectangle stood before them; the bright white light it gave off was blocked by a massive throng of bipedal creatures, all clad in various materials and holding all sorts of large objects. At least twenty of them had entered so far, and more were still filing in. There was no sign of any end to them.

The sight was horribly intimidating, and the utter fear broke Click out of their raid-fueled stupor. At least just enough for them to finally get their first good look at the intruders.

[Observation]!

Dwarf	
Name	Brimir Steelbeard
Deity	Dhevos of the Burning Anvil
Classes	Iron Mountain's Forgelord Crusader (Level 55)

Attributes	
Health	850
Body	657
Intellect	214
Soul	545

Oh . . . Oh no.

Click had a feeling of utter dread in their gut, which no other monster shared.

The hounds howled in rage-fueled confidence and charged at the intruders alongside the bats and beetles.

"Charge!" yelled the short man at the front of the group. Everyone followed with weapons raised.

Retreat! Click yelled through their Skill at the gathered spiders, which ran away alongside their leader.

The sound of yelps, whimpers, and flesh being cut echoed out behind the [Spider Army Commander] as they made their smartest decision to date.

CHAPTER TWENTY

An Unstoppable Force vs a Little Spider

Death. Death was left in their wake. Death was what invaded their home. Death was what they ran from.

Click burned through a lot of whatever fueled their Skill as they dragged the other spiders back to their home, behind the safety of the white pillars and overhanging webs. It was the only hope they had of escaping death, after all.

The [Spider Army Commander] took their place at the top of their web mega-structure, flanked by a group of hunters and a few curious web spiders. Down on the dungeon floor below, the new intruders came in droves, cleaving through any and all monsters that threatened them.

Beetles were kicked and crushed beneath hammers, bats were shot down mid-air by flying arrows or lighting that arched between them. And the dungeon hounds? Their fate was the grisliest: limbs cleaved off with precise sword strikes, heads smashed in with heavy-handed shield bashes, and bodies burned to ashes with unforgiving fireballs.

Of course, Click had no idea what any of these weapons were. To the spider, they were novel creations that brought death with an efficiency that could not be comprehended. The [Spider Army Commander] sat still as they took in the power of these terrible instruments, piecing together what they did and how they did it.

Swords made the most sense to Click, essentially elongated fangs that were sharp on the sides as well as the tip so that they could tear from any angle. Arrows were a little more complex but could still be pieced together: a thin, hard material with a sharp, fang-like end, given enough force to pierce through its target. [Ambush Spiders] could launch their webs like that, but if they could do the same with something sharp, it would hurt a lot more. And finally, there was the magic flying through the air. Click had no frame of reference for that and, in fact, didn't even know what fire and lightning were, other than that they were very dangerous.

The [Spider Army Commander]'s mind was ablaze as three different instincts and desires gripped and pulled at them. An external sensation told them to fight, while their fear told them to run away and hide. But their curiosity won out. The spider simply observed and learned.

That didn't last long, however, as the horde of intruders killed off every monster that came to greet them as they made their way deeper into the cavern.

"Glad the dungeon response to so many of us coming in together brings all the monsters out! No need to go searching for a fight; it all comes to us! So, that should be about it for this floor, aye?" shouted the man at the front. Compared to the forty or so others, he was short and stocky, but held himself taller than anyone else. His body was covered from head to toe in a thick, glimmering material that put everyone else's weapons and armor to shame. He heaved up his hammer and settled it on his shoulders with a bored grunt.

"No, sir. There's still the spider colony," the woman who had been among the first trio to enter the cavern answered him. She and the other two had quickly made their way to the larger group after the monsters' attention had been diverted.

"Why are you blathering on about 'spiders'? I've seen nary a one attacking us!" the dwarf shot back.

"That's . . . the strange thing. Over there, by the edge of the cave, there's a colony of dungeon spiders that didn't attack us when we walked by them. But . . ."

"Hmph. If you're not going to spit it out, I'll just have to take a look for myself."

The short intruder slowly trudged his way over to Click's web while the spider continued to watch in awe. It wasn't as if there was anywhere the spiders could flee to now.

"By Dhevos's beard!" the dwarf exclaimed. "I wasn't expecting something like *this* on the first floor! A complex dungeon spider colony with a singular web! These things are supposed to be as selfish as a dwarf is with their booze. How did they manage to build this thing and *share*?"

"So they're a threat, then. Let's start smashing!" exclaimed another member of the raid party. He was also part of the original trio.

"Hmm, nah. Too much trouble. If they didn't attack you or us, then they're not under the effects of any compulsion and likely not even part of the dungeon. If they wanted blood, they would've already tried ten times over. Couple of spiders probably wandered in the last time this damned place was active and decided to settle down and have kids. Wouldn't call it good real estate, but it seems to have gone surprisingly well for them."

"But they live here, don't they? I say we take a swing anyway—"

"No," the stocky man said forcefully. "Killing them wouldn't do anything to put the dungeon back to sleep. It'd just shed innocent blood."

Three of the intruders in the back, different from the original trio, suddenly shook but settled themselves down before anyone else noticed. But not before one of them let out a shout. "They're monsters! How can you say that?"

"Dhevos asks his followers to beat out the imperfections of the world and themselves on the anvil of hard work. What, pray tell, would killing a couple of spiders that were minding their own business do for the world?"

He was answered with silence.

"Very well, then. All right, lads, I'm calling the first floor clear! We need a few scouts to stay up here in case there's any unexpected activity while the rest of us continue down to sing the dungeon a lullaby. Any volunteers? We only need a single party's worth."

The men and women behind the dwarf shifted, trying their best not to garner their leader's attention.

"Not surprised. It isn't glamorous work, especially when you could be bashing in bigger monsters' heads. But if nobody wants to do it, then—"

"We'll do it!" shouted a voice from the back.

The tide of adventurers parted to reveal a trio, different from the three who had first entered the dungeon, waving back with awkward smiles. At their head was a man in chainmail and a steel helmet that hid brown hair underneath. He continued to wave well after everyone else had noted his presence.

A woman standing next to him nudged the man on the shoulder. Despite the armor, he still winced as she made contact. She had black hair and icy blue eyes, with brownish-gray robes that hugged the armor she wore underneath them.

Click thought they were seeing double for a moment. Despite the similar makeup of each trio, the one presently speaking was different from the one that had first entered the dungeon. It was a miracle the spider even noticed, as each member of the first group matched the members of the other in terms of build: two lithe creatures covered in matte material and a large lunky one encased in something shiny.

Do these invaders have some kind of obsession with the number three? They seem to love operating in threes.

"Oh, well, that's mighty kind of you three," said the dwarf.

"We're relatively novice adventurers. Only been at it for about a year," replied the second man in the group. He was clad from head to toe in brown leather that hid him better in the darkness than the woman next to him, despite her own clothes better matching the colors of the cave. "We're not ready for the lower floors yet."

"A year is longer than most adventurers stay alive." The shorter man nodded. "But with an attitude like that, I'm surprised you were sent along with everyone else here!"

The other intruders shrunk at the comment, thankful for the darkness hiding the guilt and embarrassment that would have otherwise been obvious on their faces.

"We're actually locals," replied the smaller group's leader, the man in the armor. He brushed some brown hair back underneath his helmet. "We only joined up to visit home."

"Oh! In that case, the fine folks at your hamlet are lucky to have you. All right, stay put here and use your communication piece to reach out if something goes wrong. Don't pick any big fights while you're up here either. You're only to fight the occasional straggler that might try to start something with you, not the other way around."

"Yes, sir!" the three of them shouted back.

"All right, then. Let's get this over with, everyone. Once we reach the second floor, we'll split in two and clear both that and the third floor at once. And when that's done, we'll do the same for the last two floors. Keep with your parties and try to explore every corridor or branching path you can."

Everyone nodded.

The dwarf continued. "Kill whatever hostile monster you encounter and take whatever treasure you come across. Make sure the traps in your way can't be reset. Damage the walls if you have to and overall just mess things up! As an additional bonus, I heard the townsfolk are going to cook up an entire pig for each of us once we're done! Ha!"

The intruders headed over to the slanted tunnel that held the disabled spike trap and made their way past it to the next part of the dungeon, leaving the volunteering trio by themselves.

The three stood there looking at the entrance to the second floor for a few minutes. Precisely at the four-minute mark, they turned back to the web.

Click jumped back at the glare the trio sent the spiders' way. The dwarf's presence had merely carried danger, but the looks the [Spider Army Commander] was receiving held pure hatred.

The three looked down to the bottom of the web and at the white pillars that made its base.

"So that's her, then," the brown-haired man stated. "And it only took us a year to come back for her." He clenched his fist into a ball, which began to tremble.

"Hey, we promised we would, Thamus." The leather-clad man placed a hand on his friend's shoulder. "And here we are. United at last."

"Quintus, that was only half of the promise," said the robed woman. "The other half was giving Eldia a proper funeral. And being eaten and covered by spiders isn't what she deserves."

"So how do you want to do this, Cassia?" asked Thamus, the armored man. "I don't think a simple run and grab is going to work against these guys. Maybe Plan F would?"

"Nope, we're not trying that," replied Cassia. Her icy blue eyes turned frigid while her hands began to smolder. "We're going to do this slow and steady." Flame ignited within her palms.

"I wouldn't have it any other way," the other two said and nodded.

Click's eyes widened as a gout of flame came right at them.

It is with terrible grief that we all stand here today to say goodbye to Eldia, taken before her time.

Eldia was the daughter of proud parents, a beloved citizen of Rockfort Hamlet, and most of all, Eldia was a friend. Her life was spent helping others. No task was too difficult, whether it be washing out the barns or tilling the soil. To her, it was always a quest—to scour a terrible filth from our animals' homes, or to help search for buried treasure. So it was a surprise to no one when she chose to become an adventurer.

She was an [Explorer] at heart, and even held the Class. She explored the hamlet and its surroundings, finding all sorts of plants and herbs for us to forage over the many winters, including some that saved many of your lives.

But all good things come to an end, and life is sadly one of them. Her adventures brought her to the Rockfort Dungeon, just beyond the hills, where she met her fate. Her friends who journeyed with her risked life and limb to keep her safe, yet in the end, it was she who gave her life to save theirs. They have all said that if they had a choice, it would have been the other way around. And I believe them. All of us feel the same way.

Her body is still within the dungeon, but her soul has ascended. Let her bones nourish the earth and feed generations to come. Let peace be granted to her and us all. Let Eldia . . . be happy.

**—Eulogy recited at Eldia's funeral,
one year previous**

CHAPTER TWENTY-ONE

Battle for the Web

Bright red and orange reflected off of Click's eyes as a blast of fire came flying at the web. The heat could be felt from several feet away, but the [Spider Army Commander] had been studying the strange weapon long enough to have ordered every nearby spider to get out of the way as soon as the light flared into being.

The roar of the inferno flew just past the spiders, and by some miracle, none of them were harmed. However, the bright substance did not disappear like it had earlier. It continued to thrive on the part of the webbing it had hit . . . and began to consume it and grow.

That stuff was able to annihilate all of the other monsters that faced it; there's no way any of us can survive against it! We have to run.

The fire was able to spread far before Click could get out a command, and several hunter spiders, rather than being consumed by the flames, chose to jump down. Out of the seven that jumped, two were [Web Slingers], who shot strings of webbing from their abdomens that flew out to the cavern ceiling and took hold. They fell but were kept aloft by the string that they were still attached to and arced far over the heads of the intruders. The attacking trio didn't even notice them.

The other five spiders, all more mundane hunter forms, landed with a sickening crunch but were still able to walk. Of the five that were now grounded, three of them walked over to the white pillars for protection. But the two others chose violence.

[Command Subordinates] began to slip from the two spiders, likely due to the shock they were feeling. But their sudden freedom was short-lived. The raid instinct quickly took over, and the duo charged at the much larger trio.

They didn't make it far, as a pair of long, sharp objects flew from the leather-clad man via some strange weapon he wielded and pierced the spiders' abdomens. They squirmed for several seconds before succumbing to their injuries.

"I don't think I can easily hit them with my bow while they're between Eldia's rib cage like that," said Quintus, the leather-clad archer. "Not while keeping any of them off of us."

"Just focus on keeping Eldia safe. I'll cover point," replied Thamus. He lifted up his sword and shield and brought them to the ready.

Cassia, the robed woman, looked between her two friends with mild concern. She knew how much they cared about Eldia—gods knew she did as well—but they were talking as if . . . She shook her head and dismissed the thought. "I'm going to let the web burn slowly. We don't want them all to—"

"Don't worry, we've learned our lesson," Thamus interrupted her. "Not again."

The other two nodded and stood vigilant.

Click ignored their conversation. The spider just knew that they and the rest of their tribe were in trouble, and not just because of the fire.

These invaders weren't like the predators. They didn't kill to survive; they didn't kill only for their fill. They killed for the sake of it. These intruders were here to see the total eradication of the spider tribe, and Click wouldn't have that.

First step, who am I fighting?

Human	
Name	Thamus

Deity	N/A
Class	Heavy Warrior (Level 15)

Attributes	
Health	210
Body	167
Intellect	103
Soul	145

Human	
Name	Quintus
Deity	N/A
Class	Ranger Rogue (Level 14)

Attributes	
Health	180
Body	157
Intellect	123
Soul	135

Human	
Name	Cassia
Deity	N/A
Class	Mage (Level 17)

Attributes	
Health	140
Body	90
Intellect	157
Soul	140

Skill level up! Observation (11)

Their Classes aren't as wordy as the shorter intruder. And the numbers are much smaller! Still bigger than any spider, but there are more of us. While all of our numbers might add up to more than theirs, I don't think that necessarily means we're that much stronger than them. But maybe we have a chance? Time to find out. [Command Subordinates]!

The lead spider continuously called out their Skill in quick succession. They'd used up most of their charges to keep the others from falling to the massive horde of intruders and were left with a little over a third of their total capacity. Even with [One Army, One Being], the cost was adding up after their latest commands.

That wasn't to say they were running low. Click was confident they could put up a fight, but not a very long one. So, the only way to live was to go all-in and not pull any punches, since there wouldn't be a chance after that. Besides, Click had an idea.

All spiders, into position.

Each group of [Web Slingers], team up to grab one [Bruiser Spider] and carry it up using the web slinging method those other [Web Slingers] used.

Drop the [Bruiser Spiders] so that they're aimed to fall on the invaders.

[Bruiser Spiders], as you begin to fall, activate your [Become Stone] Skill.

Only deactivate [Become Stone] after you've made contact with either the intruders or the ground.

[Shadow Spiders], activate [Sneak] and [Shadow Travel]. Then . . .

The commands came out at a dizzying pace. Click was left exhausted from cobbling their plan together so quickly and passing out complex instructions to everyone just as fast. But it wasn't for nothing.

The spiders of the tribe sprung into action. The [Web Slingers] grouped up and each took a much larger [Bruiser Spider] into their many legs as they flew into the air.

"Hey, what are they doing?" asked Thamus, looking at the swinging spiders above them with narrowed eyes. "Cassia, try to blast them down before—"

He didn't get the chance to finish his sentence.

"Oof!" gasped Cassia as a falling rock struck her in the stomach and forced the air out of her lungs. She stumbled back a few steps and almost fell but caught herself at the last second.

Direct hit! Click exclaimed.

"There are more of them," said Quintus with a grimace. He turned his bow upwards and tried shooting one of them out of the air, but the arrow bounced off of the next falling spider with nothing more than the sound of a dull scratch.

The [Ranger Rogue] tried to scoff, but the flying projectile struck him right in the face and sent him to the ground. It didn't take long for him to rise back up to his feet, but he was met with a terrible surprise.

"Those aren't rocks!" screamed Cassia as she threw a fireball onto the ground right where the projectile had landed.

Quintus didn't bother to ask her to clarify. He pulled a dagger out of his belt and slashed at the [Bruiser Spider] that was trying to climb up his armor. It took him two strikes to kill it since the spider's carapace was akin to armor—thin and heavily rusted armor, but still more than enough to resist his second-hand blade.

"These are [Bruiser Spiders]!" shouted Cassia to the other two. "There weren't any last time; the dungeon isn't a high enough level for them!"

"I thought they were supposed to be slow enough for a newbie to hit at range!" Thamus shouted back.

"It appears they've found a way around that issue," said Quintus, the only one to not raise their voice. A strange urge was keeping him quiet, a feeling that something was wrong beyond just the falling rock spiders. "And they've found a way to use their signature Skill as an attack. Falling stone projectiles aren't part of their instinct . . ."

"Our normal positioning isn't going to work," said Cassia, forcing control over her voice. "Thamus, you block them with your shield while we stand behind. You're the only one who can block projectiles like that."

Click did not stand idly by while the trio made out the situation and repositioned themselves. The [Spider Army Commander] took control of the web spiders and ordered them to weave alternate webs down to the ground, out of the line of sight of the fire wielder.

Using stalagmites and other features in the cave as cover, the web weavers followed orders and quickly laid out a bridge down to the ground, then slowly made their way down the structure. The webs were small, however, and they were only able to move at a snail's pace in single file.

Further orders came immediately after the first web spider touched down, directing them to the side, away from the adventurers and out of the battle. The spiders on the ground were now safe. Once Click realized that they were alone, the [Spider Army Commander] went down to them.

"Ha!" shouted Thamus as his sword cleaved a falling [Bruiser Spider] in two. There was a clang as the weapon met the rocky body. Hard steel won, though not without a parting dent left in the blade.

The two pieces of the spider flew wide and caused one more casualty.

"Aah, my shoulder!" Quintus shouted as he grabbed at his right arm. "That thing flew and hit me!"

"Oh, come on!" swore Cassia. "Can you still use your bow?"

The [Ranger Rogue] tried nocking an arrow but dropped it once it was only halfway pulled. "This is bad."

"We don't have a choice anymore." Thamus looked back at his two companions grimly. "We're doing it. Plan F."

"You can't be serious, Thamus." Cassia glared back at him.

"That's Eldia over there. We have to save her! What kind of friends are we if we don't? Come on, Quintus. Are you with me?"

"Thamus." The blue in Cassia's eyes turned outright frigid as she intensified her glare. "Eldia is dead. We *already* failed to save her. I'm not going to let you die too."

"Why can't you let me redeem myself?" the [Heavy Warrior] shouted back. "What else am I supposed to do now? Her parents still mourn her, and we finally have a chance to at least bring back what's left of her so she can get a proper funeral!"

"Thamus," Quintus said to him slowly. His eyes were bleary yet sharp, as if he had suddenly sobered up after a night of drinking. "If we let you die, how are *we* supposed to redeem *ourselves*?"

"... I didn't think about that," Thamus huffed. "I—"

Before he could finish his sentence, a terrible prick of pain flared to life on his neck.

[Shadow Spiders], start biting! shouted Click in their head.

"Oh gods, what's going on?" shouted Thamus as he slapped at the source of the pain. He didn't find anything but felt another bite soon after. And then another and another.

"[Shadow Spiders]!" exclaimed Cassia as she slapped at her own robes. "They must've hitched a ride on the falling [Bruiser Spiders]! There's no other way they could've snuck up on us!"

"Screw it! I'm raising the alarm!" screamed Thamus as he put a finger to his ear and called out. "We're under attack! The spiders are aggressive!" A second later, the [Heavy Warrior] gave the others a shaky thumbs-up between the pain.

"Hey, if help is coming, maybe we should go with Plan F anyway?"

Thamus and Quintus looked over to Cassia and readied themselves to shoot down any possible objection she might've raised. Instead, the only thing she brought up was a rolled-up sheet of parchment.

Pain from the venomous bites still rang through her body, but the [Mage] forced herself to unfurl the scroll and start reading from its contents. The strange glyphs on the page began to glow blue and emanate wisps of magical energy that lashed out at everything around it.

Even Click could feel the force of the raw magic whipping against them, and while they didn't know what it was, it gave them a very bad feeling.

The [Spider Army Commander] ordered their troops to double down on the attack and bite down even harder. They did as they were instructed, but the size difference between them and their targets was too great, and their targets only flinched at each attack.

And suddenly, the magic halted. The entire cavern was dead silent as every sentient creature looked on in trepidation. Click's bad feeling worsened.

"Fireball!" Cassia shouted as the scroll began to glow red hot, then reformed into a blazing orange ball and launched itself at the web with a terrible scream. The hundreds of hunter and web spiders still on the mega-structure could do nothing as the flaming ball connected and instantly detonated.

The entire web was turned into a blazing conflagration, and a massive pressure wave threw what few spiders hadn't instantly been turned to ash across the cave. The lucky ones hit a rock or other hard surface and immediately splattered into goop. The unlucky ones caught on fire and slowly burned to death as they futilely ran in circles before collapsing.

Then there were the miracle cases. A few of the smaller spiders, juveniles and some remaining [Shadow Spiders], were caught by the [Web Slingers]. Some landed on top of the soft corpse of a predator or bat, and a few of the web spiders had already made it down from the web before the fireball hit. But that wasn't to say the tribe was safe. Almost everyone was dead.

As Click watched the devastation, unable to conjure a single coherent thought, Thamus charged into the flaming pile, grabbed the white pillars, dragged them back to his other party members, and fell to the ground with them.

"We did it," the intruder said weakly. "We saved her. We saved Eldia." *My home . . .*

CHAPTER TWENTY-TWO

Battle for the Web: Conclusion

Revenge. It's a very controversial topic. There exist myths and legends that glorify the act, while history and common teachings decry it. It seems that everyone has an opinion on the subject.

A very common story that many myths tell is that of a revenge seeker, who has unjustly suffered at the hands of a terrible evil and is thus led on a quest to become powerful enough to defeat them. The hero, of course, eventually wins and takes their place as the villain's successor, with implications that they will rule more justly.

More recent history, on the other hand, shows that things tend to go differently. And never well. Either the revenge seeker, blinded by rage, makes a foolhardy mistake early on that spells their demise, or they become far worse, in pursuit of their goal, than whatever villain they were attempting to vanquish.

This scholar has yet to read accurate accounts of a revenge tale gone right, let alone seen one with their own eyes. Perhaps there will soon be a case where the quest for revenge is successful or, perhaps, where the hero finds a more constructive goal with a similar end result?

**—Tavern talk by Rogulus Dragonlove,
bard and historian**

The last few moments played out in Click's mind in slow motion.

Ash, flaming webs, and the charred remains of hundreds of spiders flew across the cave as Thamus collapsed next to his companions.

The noise and shockwave completely blindsided Click, who was left too stunned to properly respond.

As burning pieces of webbing collected on Thamus's armor, turning it red hot, the intruder grabbed the white pillars of the spiders' home and pulled with all his might. A newfound desperate will coursed through his body and seemed to muffle the burning in his arms and on his skin as he heaved the bones of his old friend out of the ground. Fire continued to rain down around him as he turned around and ran back to his companions with the corpse held in his arms in a tight hug. Thamus collapsed as soon as he made it back to safety.

"W-we did it," the adventurer mumbled from his place on the cavern floor.

"We got her back," added Quintus with a weary smile.

"More than worth it," said Cassia in between deep, labored breaths.

M-my home . . . Click thought. *They took my home. They killed all of my brethren . . . They destroyed . . . everything.* The spider lost all feeling in their legs and felt them begin to curl up.

The intruders all wept tears, both bitter and sweet. If spiders could cry, Click's tears would have only been bitter. A series of new feelings erupted within Click, something with an intensity they had never felt before. It was gut wrenching. Grief and rage, both at a level the [Spider Army Commander] had never felt before, blazed inside them.

They had experienced a kind of loss that, until now, had been utterly incomprehensible. To lose everything all at once. Click felt . . . *hatred.* These intruders were going to suffer.

[Command Subordinates]. Start biting.

The [Shadow Spiders] that were still on the adventurers snapped out of their stupor and began their attack anew. Venom-drenched fangs pierced unprotected skin as lithe legs carried the stealth attackers to other parts of the intruders' bodies before they could react.

But none of the intruders *were* reacting. They had already fallen to their knees or onto their backsides and were just staring at the black sockets set within the strangely shaped top piece of the spiders' home with melancholy smiles—the top piece that Click was beginning to realize resembled the intruders' heads.

Idle wonder casually passed through the spider's mind as they called up their Skill once more.

[Command Subordinates]. Faster. Bite harder. Kill them.

The spiders obliged, yet the intruders didn't react. However, in the dim light of the glowing mushrooms, their faces began to turn ever so slightly pale.

"That scroll took too much out of me, guys. More than I even had to begin with," grunted Cassia. "Got too much mana burn to even reach for a potion, let alone swat this spider off of me."

"Don't worry, Cassia. You're not the only one," Quintus replied in a drawn-out breath. "I think the venom's starting to take effect anyway, so it's not like you would've been able to do much either way. Can't even get my armor off to find them because of my sprained shoulder. I think it might even be broken. Three [Shadow Spiders] on us each is too much. Ugh."

"Three? It's just one for me," said the [Mage].

"Oh. Well, what about you, Thamus?"

". . . Thamus?"

The armored man was frozen in place, his eyes still staring into the empty eyes of his friend. The vibrancy of life was still visible within his own eyes, just a spark, but it was slowly fading. The chainmail on his back still gave off smoke and had sunk a fraction of an inch into his skin.

"Oh gods, how much damage did you take, Thamus? Your armor's melted into your flesh!" Quintus let out a weak cough before falling.

Thamus didn't respond.

Good.

Click didn't need to be human to understand what despair looked like. The spider knew these three were feeling it, feeling the same emotion they had inflicted upon Click.

Before the [Spider Army Commander] could bask any further in the intruders' suffering, a faraway noise broke them out of their stupor. That noise soon revealed itself to be the crunching of boots on the cave floor.

"I got the alert and heard an explosion! What's wrong?" shouted the dwarf, with dozens of others just behind him.

"S-spiders, [Shadow . . .]," muttered Quintus before fully collapsing. "In our armor."

The shorter adventurer didn't hesitate and snapped at another robed woman standing near him. "You, hydromancer lass! Make them wet! Make sure the water seeps all the way through their armor and onto their skin!"

"B-but what wou—"

"DO IT!"

The standing [Mage] didn't argue back and simply pointed her hands at the downed trio. A blast of water flew at them, almost immediately drenching them from head to toe.

"Now freeze them!"

"Into a solid block? I'm not a high enough level to—"

"Just a little. Bring them as close to water's freezing point as you can." The dwarf took a deep breath and tried to calm himself. "Please."

The hydromancer nodded and complied without another word. A chill resonated from her hands and blew through the cavern, leaving a trail of small ice crystals over the leftover puddles of water as it passed by. When the chill reached the adventurers, their clothes and exposed skin began to frost over. Cloth stiffened while leather formed a layer of ice over its surface. Underneath the fabrics and armors, ice began to form just above their skin and, soon enough, enveloped the [Shadow Spiders], which were forced to stop their assault.

The dwarf didn't give the standing [Mage] a chance to pause her attack; he rushed over to the downed trio with several vials in hand. Three small glasses filled with a deep red liquid were placed to each of the adventurers' mouths, and they were forced to imbibe the contents.

"Easy now. It's a healing potion. Can't exactly do triage when you're seconds away from dying, now, can I?" The dwarf let out a small chuckle. "We don't exactly have antivenom, but dungeon spider venom should pass through your systems within a few days."

"Th-thank you," coughed Quintus. "Thamus ran through a fire and Cassia's got mana burn."

"Well, you heard him! Get them a burn and mana potion each!" shouted the shorter man at the other adventurers standing by.

A pyromancer and their teammate rushed over to bring Thamus and Cassia each a drink from their own belts.

After drinking them, Thamus only blinked while Cassia slowly and dizzily lifted herself up to her feet.

"So, now that you three aren't going to die, would you mind telling me why I shouldn't report you to the Adventurer's Guild and have you all thrown in jail?" The shorter adventurer's nurturing expression turned both fiery and frigid as he glared at the trio.

"Jail?" asked one of the adventurers in the back of the crowd.

"Didn't they get attacked?" mumbled another.

"Yeah, they threw up the emergency alarm."

Even the offending trio looked confused.

The dwarf pointed at the skeleton before them and shouted, "Dungeon ossium! You greedy fools brought this upon yourselves. I saw that corpse underneath the spider's web. I'm not an idiot. I know you attacked them first if you have that!"

"Hold on. What's 'ossium'?" asked a voice from the crowd.

Before the group could erupt into a mumble of questions, the lead adventurer spoke up. "It's a substance that forms in dungeons. When bones are subjected to a dungeon's magical energies, they become incredibly hard, akin to gemstones. They're worth their weight in gems because of their enchantability and their sheer beauty."

"So, how are they in that much trouble for wanting some?" another voice asked. "They're just bones; it's not like they're rare or anything."

The dwarf's left eye twitched, but he bit down on his anger. Most of it, anyway. "Monster bones don't work, since they're already attuned to the dungeon, and animal bones will attune before the process completes. So think about it, genius. What does that leave you with?"

"H-human bones?" someone weakly asked.

"Or that of any of the Noble Races. And I'm sure you all know what happens when you mix money and death. You get murder. Followed by regulations from the Adventurer's Guild and *punishments* for breaking them. That's not to mention what Dhevos's opinion on the matter is." The dwarf's eyes were especially fiery as he made that final statement.

But as he continued to look at the three, especially Thamus, his gaze began to soften. He saw the party's leader still staring at the corpse's eye sockets, almost as unblinkingly as the skull. A single tear fell from his eye into its head.

"What's her name?" he finally asked.

"Eldia," replied Thamus, not even looking away.

"You loved her, lad?"

"Yeah."

The other two party members looked at their friend with wide eyes.

"I—I didn't even . . . ," mumbled Cassia.

Quintus tried to school his expression but underneath it something was roiling: regret and personal failure. ". . . meant that much to you? We didn't do enough . . ."

"What in the thousand hells are you talking about, lad?" shouted the dwarf, breaking everyone out of their stupor. "You got the girl back. What more *is* there to do? But why didn't you tell me in the first place?"

"You said it yourself: gathering dungeon ossium is illegal," said Cassia, shrugging. "We figured you'd think we were only after her for the money, not because she's our friend. I mean, that's the kind of thing all of these other adventurers would try to pull."

The crowd behind the shorter man collectively glared at Cassia.

"Oh, knock it off, you lot," said the dwarf, turning around to give them all the stink eye. "You're all *absolutely* the kind of fools who'd try to pull that kind of thing! That's why you were dragged along on this job in the first place."

The adventurers broke eye contact and looked down in embarrassment.

The shorter man faced the trio again and cleared his throat. "Right, then. After your emergency alarm and the explosion, I grabbed everyone and ran back up here. With everything so sidetracked, we'll have to regroup and continue the raid tomorrow. Otherwise, the dungeon might get wise to what we're all doing and try to cut its losses with this active season. Besides, we got just enough done today that we can hit it even harder tomorrow and get it to close down for even longer. I just hope the townsfolk will be fine with accommodating us for an extra day because of your actions."

The trio looked at each other, then back to their leader.

"Since you helped bring Eldia back to them, I wouldn't be surprised if they invited you all to stay for another year," said Thamus.

"Now that's the Thamus we know!" exclaimed Cassia as she walked over and hugged her friend.

Quintus, blushing red after being given an offer to join them, slowly made his way over and joined in the group embrace.

As the adventurers looked at each other with happy eyes, a small figure in the shadows looked beyond them with weariness.

Click dragged themself into the distance towards the sliced corpse of the [Alpha Hound] and summoned their Skill.

[Command Subordinates]. If you're alive and can safely move, come down here.

A [Shadow Spider] crawled out of the bisected creature's fur and stopped in front of the [Spider Army Commander].

A [Web Slinger] from up high slowly descended from a stalactite and let go of its web about a foot from the ground. It landed in front of its leader.

An oblong rock off to the side suddenly came to life and walked over on its seven legs and stump, settling on its belly in front of Click.

They weren't *all* dead. Click raised a leg into the air, and the fifteen spiders behind them did the same, with the three newcomers wordlessly following along. They had survived. Hope wasn't lost. They would rebuild. And that in itself was a victory.

The large door at the end of the cavern creaked shut as the intruders left the dungeon, and a notification popped up in Click's vision.

> Raid status: Failure! +0 Experience

Click narrowed their eyes but stood tall. It was still a victory, even if *someone* didn't think the same. But if that someone really thought so poorly of the spiders, then they didn't matter. Not in the slightest.

CHAPTER TWENTY-THREE

Rebuilding

So what puts adventurers above monsters in strength? What makes them "greater"? I don't mean in terms of a specific matchup, but overall. Wait, I already know your answer: it's the System, isn't it? Sure, it's not a bad answer per se, but don't monsters also have access to it?

What's that you're about to say? The Noble Races have access to their own version of the System, which makes us better? No, it makes us more versatile. I'd like to see a level forty [Baker] square up against a [Desolation Engine] and walk out of it as anything other than a red smear.

So then, what is it? I bet you're dying for me to tell you, but only if—okay, fine! Sheesh.

It's civilization. Adventurers don't rush into battles buck naked with only their fists. They have armor, weapons, potions, and spell scrolls for the more advanced forms of magic they can't cast on the fly. And unlike monsters, they don't have to make or grow everything they use from scratch.

How much of a monster's System attributes, biology, and Skills are devoted to growing their own armor? And how much of what's left over is devoted to thinking well? How about us? How much of our bodies and Skills are devoted to growing thick armor out of our skin? You've got the [Armored Skin] Skill? Well, what good is that when you wear a layer of metal over your skin that'll protect you even better and that doesn't hog up a Skill, which would otherwise be more useful?

So yeah, civilization. It's what really got us so far, and it's why we're top dog.

—Anonymous banter between a drunk royal scholar and an adventuring party, overheard at a tavern

Revenge?

Click didn't have time for that. The spider most certainly wanted to take part in it, but with almost the entire tribe dead and their home now a smoldering ruin, Click had slightly more pressing matters to attend to. Such as not starving to death and finding safety from whatever monsters had also survived the adventurers' wrath. Even the [Spider Army Commander] was smart enough to not place their feelings above staying alive.

A day passed, and the arachnid survivors of the dungeon massacre set themselves up on the ceiling of the cavern, away from the prying eyes of the intruders, who had come back for another round of bloodshed. With almost all of the bats killed off, there was plenty of free real estate available. However, there was one small problem.

Where are all the flies? Click shouted to themself in frustration. The nascent mega-web the spider sat in was almost completely white, with the exception of the few spiders that called it home. A [Bruiser Spider] trundled over to a black speck in the web and stuck its mandibles into it. It didn't even bother to chew the morsel as it tossed it into their mouth and swallowed it whole. It looked unsatisfied.

Click relaxed their legs and began to curl up, the spider equivalent of a sigh. *We don't have any choice, then. Time for a hunting trip.*

The others could feel the shift in their leader and immediately brightened up.

Don't get your hopes up. I'm not bringing a crowd down just to get us all killed again. Click used [Command Subordinates] and pointed out several of the smallest spiders, mostly [Shadow Spiders] and [Web Slingers] with a single [Bruiser Spider] to carry back their food.

The others looked back at their leader with disappointment, but they didn't do much.

[Command Subordinates]. Wait here, don't pick any fights with the intruders down below, and we'll bring you back plenty to eat.

That made the others light up.

Click and the rest of the chosen party departed the web, slowly crawling down the side of the cave until they made it to the floor behind several rocks. There were no webs to make their descent any easier, as any new ones would have alerted the intruders.

The [Spider Army Commander] wasn't scared that the other spiders would pick a fight with the strange and powerful creatures either. After the disaster yesterday, a blanket of melancholy had fallen upon all of the spiders, even the less intelligent ones. It was as if a brand-new instinct cloyed at them—one that simply pervaded every aspect of their existence, like a choking miasma, rather than grabbing their reins.

When the call of the raid came, the spiders weren't as excited to jump into action. It made wrangling them easier, and Click was confident that [Command Subordinates] would keep them under control for an extended period of time. But the lead spider felt this was too good to be true and that there was somehow something more to the feeling.

Click put the feeling aside and made their way between rocks and stalagmites alongside their stealthy brethren, careful to avoid the wandering gazes of any intruders. All the while, the spiders took the opportunity to grab at any flies they passed by. With the death of so many monsters, there were bound to be plenty of insects flying around soon enough, but everyone needed to eat *now.*

"So what happened to those three from yesterday?" asked a passing adventurer. Her eyes fell as her head turned on a slow swivel. "We're taking their job, after all. I'd like to know why."

"I overheard one of the villagers this morning," began another adventurer. His gaze was sharper as his eyes darted all around the cave, but he still missed Click. "The venom was pretty bad, so they're still recovering. They'll probably be bedridden for another month unless they find a really good healer."

"Are there even any healers out here? Maybe an herbalist or something, though I doubt they'd be as good."

"It's not like they could afford it anyway, especially since they gave that dungeon ossium or whatever up to that family." His lips curled up into a sneer.

"Yeah, really dumb move," the other adventurer scoffed.

Click didn't know what the two were talking about, but something about their tone rubbed the spider the wrong way. It was careless, irreverent, and downright annoying, like the intruders that had attacked the spiders' home yesterday. The spider didn't want to spend more time around them and continued past. If Click hadn't, they would've attacked the invaders instead.

Eventually, the hunting party reached the edge of the cave and the corridor that led to some new, unknown place. Many of the intruders were going there, and for all Click knew, there would be new food down there—bigger, juicier, and producing more experience. The intruders had dragged the monsters they'd killed out of the cavern and done who knew what with them; off the menu went many would-be easy meals. The next best hope for such a feast was down another level.

The spider shook their head. Of course, that was all speculation and wasn't likely true. But with everything that had happened, the [Spider Army Commander] was beginning to feel like there wasn't as much to lose. While melancholy ruled most of their mind, curiosity was able to take control of what was left and guided Click past the trap and down onto the second floor of the dungeon.

It was pretty much the same. The same rocks, in both color and size, the same scattering of stalagmites, and . . .

"*Hwoooreee!*" came a screech from the distance.

Click and the other spiders ran to the nearest wall and began to climb until they were perched halfway to the ceiling.

Below them, a group of strange creatures that looked similar to the predators howled as they charged at four intruders. The creatures walked with four legs and were covered in thick, matted fur, and they had snouts that tapered off into a flat nose with two holes and a pair of sharp tusks that came up on either side.

[Observation]!

Dungeon Boar (Level 10)	
Soul Link	Rockfort Hamlet Dungeon Core [????????]
Classes	N/A

Evolution Prerequisites	
Species	Juvenile Dungeon Boar

Attributes	
Health	35
Body	25
Intellect	11
Soul	15

Level 9: Running Charge
Increase speed when moving in a straight, unobstructed line.

Level 23: Scent Tracking
Track a target by its scent over great distances and amongst other scents.

Level 15: Iron Fangs
Teeth are reinforced to be harder and sharper. Bites do not heal as easily.

Click saw that it was an adult version of the evolution chain, at least according to the evolutionary structure that other monsters followed, and even recognized two out of the three Skills. [Scent Tracking] was interesting, but it likely didn't have much use beyond finding prey.

"Come on, right over here!" came a shout from where the dungeon boar was facing.

Click and the porcine monster both looked towards its source and saw an intruder taunting the boar. The monster didn't give a second thought before running at him.

"Too slow!" the intruder shouted before quickly juking to the side. "Try again!"

The monster took the challenge and ran once more, only for the adventurer to jump out of the way again.

What's this idiot doing? If this intruder is as strong as the ones from yesterday, he should be able to kill the dungeon boar easily. Click watched in frustration as the man continued to jump and dive out of the way of the monster's useless attacks.

Frustration soon turned to disappointment at both of the parties and finally to rage as the adventurer's taunts had a second-hand effect. *Just stab that idiot with your tusks already!*

Click had to control themself from jumping down into the battle and biting the intruder or having the other spiders weave a web to trip him up. The [Spider Army Commander] wasn't foolish enough to pull off a suicide attack or to get the adventurer's attention, but they had to exert more self-control than usual to stop themself.

Wait a minute . . . [Observation].

Click focused the Skill on the intruder and was greeted with a slightly different menu than expected.

Level 16: Dodge
Avoid enemy attacks with a swift movement at the last moment.

Level 14: Sneak
Shadows and obstacles better conceal you from others, visually and sonically.

Level 12: Shadow Travel
Move much more quickly while concealed in darkness or shadow.

Level 3: Critical Strike
When the enemy is unaware, deal additional damage to weak points.

The adventurer quickly looked at a ring on their hand before focusing back on the battle before them.

Only a Skill list? And the way they looked at their ring right as I used my Skill . . . Maybe it's supposed to warn about or stop [Observation]? Maybe it stops me from getting their attributes, but they're not actively preventing me from reading them, so I'm still able to get their Skills? Makes sense. These fools only know how to swing their weapons around and pick fights; they probably don't have brains!

Click clamped down on their thoughts, forcing their rage under control once more. It was the third time that had happened today. It wasn't as if it was some sort of [Taunt] Skill; the [Spider Army Commander]'s anger was caused by their own sensibilities.

As much as Click wanted to seek vengeance, they knew that even trying would invite death; the spider *hated* that they had to keep looking at these horrible intruders. Their brand-new idiocy didn't help either.

"And there we go. Level ups all over!" the adventurer cheered.

Click couldn't understand what they said but could understand the joy in their voice. Either that, or it was some sort of battle cry. *[Observation].*

Level 17: Dodge
Avoid enemy attacks with a swift movement at the last moment.

Level 14: Sneak
Shadows and obstacles better conceal sight and sound from others.

Level 13: Shadow Travel
Move much more quickly while concealed in darkness or shadow.

Level 3: Critical Strike
When the enemy is unaware, deal additional damage to weak points.

[Dodge] and [Shadow Travel] both increased, huh? Maybe that was what the intruder was trying to do, after all.

"Hey, Felix, want to finish this up?" came a higher pitched voice from further into the cave. "I've got my own Skills I want to level."

"Yeah, sure!" the dodging adventurer answered. "Hey, everyone, guide your boars to the center!"

A few more squeals could be heard from just a bit further in the cave, and a few more lithe adventurers with their own dungeon boar escorts ran towards a central point. The boars, hot on their trails, continued their charge until they were all within a few feet of each other.

At first, Click was sure the intruders were trying to guide the monsters into impaling each other with their tusks, but the beasts proved too smart for that and slowed to a trot as they got close. But before any of the dungeon boars could break out of their little group in another charge, the adventurers disappeared.

The monsters looked around in confusion before sticking their noses up into the air and sniffing around.

Crack!

A small clear-colored hollow vessel containing a brown liquid sailed through the air from the hands of another adventurer and shattered as it hit the floor. The liquid inside spilled forth, and as soon as the dungeon boars took a whiff, they froze.

"*Hwoooreee!*" they all screamed as they began to charge pell-mell in all directions.

The air from the site of the attack wafted over, and Click could smell something terrible in it. The boars down on the ground could too, apparently, and it was much worse for them for some reason . . .

It's [Scent Tracking]! Click shouted to themself in surprise. *Those intruders used it against them as a weapon!*

The dungeon boars began to run around in circles, heedless of their surroundings and each other—and of the adventurers who jumped out and began to attack.

A series of quick stabs at vital spots put the creatures down quickly, and the intruders began to cheer.

"And there's another level up for [Critical Strike]! Can't believe I only got it yesterday too!"

The intruders patted themselves on the back a little bit more before heading further into the cavern. With the way clear, Click and the other spiders descended from their spots on the wall and ran over to the slain dungeon boars to feast.

As the [Spider Army Commander] finally filled their stomach and eased the worst of their anger, their old rage was slowly replaced with something brand new.

How did they do that? Click excitedly thought. *Those intruders had a plan laid out and executed it perfectly! None of them seemed to be using [Command Subordinates] since they were all acting the same the entire time. It's as if they were instructed well before they entered the dungeon.*

What Click felt was akin to curiosity, but there was more to it; excitement, joy, and wonder filled their mind as they continued to think about the strange intruders.

Those strange noises they were making . . . With how complex they were, maybe they had meaning in them? Could they have used those to communicate?

Another bite, another bit of rage subsided, and another thought.

And that stink! What was that item that contained it? I've never seen anything like it. Did they make it? I doubt they have the natural biology to do it, like we do for webs, so maybe they found it lying around? No, it was too precise. Just like our webs, they must have made it somehow. But did one of them make it? Spiders have hunters and web weavers; maybe they have members who only craft things for their hunters? But how did they make it? I can't even begin to imagine!

Thoughts and ideas continued to flood Click's mind, and the feeling of awe for these strange intruders began to rise. If Click could harness that power, then the spider tribe would be unstoppable! Almost all of the anger from before had evaporated or, rather, had transformed into a desire to learn. A desire to learn from the intruders' strength and apply it so that they would never harm Click or the tribe again.

Prerequisites acquired for evolution
Evolution acquired for Class

Error: Class incompatible with Monster
Error: Monster incompatible with Class
Error: Monster incompatible with Monster
Error: Soul Link incompatible with Soul
Error

. . .

. . .

Click was beginning to feel dizzy and had to stop themself from vomiting their meal.

. . .

Prerequisite Achieved! Unlocked Class: Anthropologist
Skill obtained: Decipher Language

That . . . was weird.

Click didn't know what had happened but felt something strange going on within them. After sating themself on dungeon boar, the spider instructed the [Spider Bruiser] to carry some leftovers back to the other survivors.

Thankfully, they didn't encounter any of the intruders along the way and were able to easily avoid the two who were guarding the first floor with minimal effort.

"Man, I wish we would find some good treasure up here. Do you think there are any other old human corpses around?" asked one of the guards.

The other one looked at their partner and glared. "Don't even think about it. Brimir will turn your head into a smear on the wall before you even get halfway through my Health."

"Woah, I wasn't thinking anything!"

"Sure, you weren't. And even if you did manage it, you'd have to wait like a year before my bones would transform."

Click scoffed again as they passed by the pair. *If those idiots actually do try to kill each other, then it would make my life easier. Maybe I should do something to tempt them along?*

The [Spider Army Commander] stopped in place and opened their eyes wide. *Wait, how did I know they were talking about killing each other?*

Skill level up! Decipher Language (2)
Class level up! Anthropologist (2)

The brand-new Skill already had some use! Click was happy for that, but they still didn't understand what this "Class" was. Asking the System didn't give any more information on it either, so the spider was still in the dark.

Whatever. It doesn't get in the way of my ability to lead my brethren and survive.

Soon enough, Click was back in their makeshift web and calling their Skill to alert the others still stationed there.

[Command Subordinates]. Food is here! Come eat!

Click waited for several seconds, but nobody came to meet them. The other spiders that had just returned looked around in confusion before deciding to follow Click's command and dig into the food they had brought back.

Click quickly commanded them to stop and wait for the others, which they hesitantly followed, but even after another minute nobody appeared.

What's going on? Where is everyone? Click began to explore the mega-web in impatience and soon found the answer.

In a dark corner of the web, a small basket had been woven together, which held the corpses of the remaining spiders. And among them was a pile of eggs. The same kind of eggs that Click and the other spiders had first hatched out of.

They mated! I told them to stay here and not pick a fight, so they decided to mate and lay eggs instead! I can't say I blame them, but WHY ARE THEY ALL DEAD?

The concept of mating existed within Click's mind. They could pair up with any other dungeon spider variant, and the process was supposed to feel good and produce eggs that would hatch into new baby spiders. But that didn't say anything about dying!

In hindsight, it made sense. If that instinct did come with such a warning, then it would conflict with their need for survival and they would never make new spiders. But why did the other spiders choose to do it now, instead of any other time?

Click figured it out in an instant. *It's because the entire tribe's almost dead. It must be a brand-new instinct! Everyone's been feeling weird recently. But after seeing these eggs, I'm starting to feel a little bit better. A little happy. This tribe isn't dead, and we'll rise back up!*

The cloud of melancholy began to lift from Click, as well as from the others. But with this newfound hope, old habits and instincts returned.

The other spiders immediately jumped or ran out of the web, making a beeline for the two intruders patrolling the cavern floor.

No! [Command Subordinates]! Get back here, you idiots!

CHAPTER TWENTY-FOUR

Finding Something Productive to Do

Having a good second-in-command, not to mention a proper command hierarchy, is essential to running any kind of operation where the work alone isn't motivating enough to captivate your workers. In the case of war especially, nobody wants to actually fight and die if they can help it. So if the leader is rendered incapable of performing their duties, unless there is someone to take their place, things will descend into chaos.

Take the Johovian Conflict from some time ago. A very common strategy of the Shostran Army was to target the opposing side's army leaders. It was discovered early on in the war that, apparently, many of the Johovian troops were uninterested civilians who had been drafted and, thus, weren't all too keen on fighting.

To combat this, the Johovians had specialized [Control Commanders] leading their battalions. These commanders had dedicated Skills that kept their troops under control and prevented insurrection. So when one of these [Control Commanders] was taken out, their troops would inevitably rebel or surrender to us!

What's funny is that something similar happened to us a generation ago. During the Vanara wars, our troops were forced to fight in the dense, hot, and humid jungles of the west. Combined with the fact that it was a war of pride, rather than of actual value, this led to record low enlistment and, subsequently, the institution of a draft.

But the Vanaras didn't have to target our commanders. We did it ourselves! Our own generals and commanders pushed our troops past their limits, to the point where some of them decided that if death was inevitable, they might as well target the real enemy. We lost many officers as a result while the chain of command fell apart.

So, while the moral of both of these stories is to establish a better chain of command, perhaps the real lesson is to treat your troops well?

—Excerpt from an interview with Magnus Silvershell, retired general of the Shostran Army

Poke.

An errant leg jabbed Click in the side, and the spider ignored it.

Poke. Poke.

Click was pretty sure that the leg wasn't so errant after all.

Poke. Poke. Poke.

All right! the lead spider shouted in their head while waving the jabs away.

While the [Spider Army Commander] had leveled [Command Subordinates] enough that they could keep the remaining spiders under full control near-indefinitely without running out of charge, the Skill couldn't control how the others felt.

And right now . . .

Poke.

They felt bored.

"Oh my gods, I'm so bored!" came a shout from below them. One of the intruders threw their arms in the air with a growl before taking a deep breath. "Seriously, you'd think they'd be done by now!"

Skill level up! Decipher Language (3)

Click was starting to wrap their head around the idea that these intruders communicated through the complex noises they made, and their newfound Skill allowed them to piece together the general meaning of what the intruders were talking about through context clues. Which was quite strange to the spider, considering that those context clues were just as foreign.

But from what Click could understand, they agreed with the intruder. It was probably the only thing they agreed on.

"If you're so bored, then find something to fight, or whatever. There are still a few Baby Dungeon Hounds running around."

"And give you the chance to let me get killed so you can make dungeon ossium out of my corpse? As if!"

"For the last time, I *can't* get away with doing that, and even if I tried, I'd go to jail for life! Or even be executed!"

The other adventurer scoffed and looked away, moving their hand closer to their sword.

Skill level up! Decipher Language (4)

Click rolled their eyes, or at least managed the spider equivalent. These two were beginning to get as annoying as—

Poke.

All right, fine! Click shouted to themself while raising their front two arms in the air, mimicking the intruder below. *These eggs can't hatch on the ceiling, unless we want all of our niblings to go splat as soon as they hatch, but we can't lower them while these two idiots are walking around.*

The spiders looked at their leader with curiosity. Maybe they'd finally gotten through?

Click called over a [Web Slinger] and had them take point at the edge of their web.

This particular spider had a talent for aiming thanks to their [3D Move Sense], no doubt, but there was more to it: they were just a natural.

Shoot some webbing into the fur on top of its head. It seems to groom it a lot, so that should be a bit of a bother. But don't go down there to make contact or anything. Just shoot a single glob.

The [Web Slinger] followed through without complaint and launched an orb of webbing at the adventurer. It landed on her hair without her noticing, and after a few moments, she brushed at it.

"What the thousand? Did you put this in my hair?" she accused the other adventurer.

"Put what?"

"This spider web! Was it from the nest that those three burned down yesterday?"

As the two continued to bicker, Click felt a twinge of inspiration. The [Excretion Launcher] Skill said that it could launch any bodily substance, and all of the [Web Slingers] were instinctually using it to shoot webbing. But what about venom?

Shoot some of your venom into its mouth.

The spider complied and landed a light stream of the toxic substance right on top of her tongue.

"Well, you were—*blech!*" The adventurer began to cough as she tried to spit it out. "Was that a fly or something? That tasted awful!"

The other adventurer just shrugged and took the opportunity to end the conversation.

A few moments passed, and the intruder began to look a little pale. "I don't think my stomach feels too great . . . Wait, I think that was poison. Hey! Did you try to poison me?"

"What? How could I even do that from over here?"

"I know you did! Maybe with some kind of poison sprayer? That would explain the weird taste in my mouth!" She pulled out her sword. "I'm not letting you kill me. Let's go!"

"Woah, what are you—"

She charged.

Click and the other spiders watched with mild interest as the two idiots fought. Weapons collided and blood was drawn, but both were evenly matched. It wasn't so much the raw skill of the combatants that brought everyone entertainment as it was the sight of a couple of nuisances getting themselves hurt.

Sadly, the fun didn't last long. A series of loud footsteps echoed out from just beyond the corridor to the second floor, and a small group of people ran in, shouting.

"What do you two idiots think you're doing?" shouted the one in front, a woman with orange hair tied into a tight bun.

"He poisoned me!" shouted one of the combatants.

"Did not! I was minding my own business, and she just accused me!"

"I don't care who did what; you both had a job and you're trying to kill each other instead of doing it! Get out of here! Head back to town and stay put until the rest of us are done."

"But—" both of them started.

"How are you two even supposed to be on the same team? I just . . . No more words. Get out."

The two gave the woman a crestfallen look and slowly trudged their way out.

"By the gods," she sighed as soon as they'd left, then looked to the small group behind her. "You three, you're taking over for them. Guard the floor and call us if you're attacked or anything strange happens."

The trio nodded and took their places, standing far enough apart from each other that they could cover most ground with their sight but still rush to each other's aid if needed. They looked to be much more attentive than the previous duo, and now Click was certain they couldn't get away with the same stunt.

While the other spiders fell back into their depressive stupor, the [Spider Army Commander] only lit up.

They got replaced so quickly? And where's the short one? They didn't give any orders—just that taller one over there did! There must be some kind of chain of command, with this new intruder in charge of matters that aren't important enough for the short one.

Click looked over to the other spiders on the web, then back to the intruders' apparent second-in-command. The spider performed the equivalent of a shrug and looked to the dungeon exit and the angry shouting that could be heard from outside, then finally back to the other spiders.

Yeah, it's going to take some time before they're ready to lead. Maybe if they take some kind of leadership-oriented evolution soon—or at least one that increases their intelligence.

Skill level up! Decipher Language (5)
Class level up! Anthropologist (3)

Well, I doubt these new intruders are going to leave for a while, so maybe it's time for another trip? I might as well continue observing the intruders and, hopefully, find a way to get them to leave sooner. But in the meantime, I could at least try to learn more about their organizational structure and how to eventually apply it to my own tribe. Having some sub-leaders would make things much easier for me.

[Command Subordinates]. Come on! It's time for another "hunting trip."

The spiders all perked up and lined up to follow their leader down deeper into the cavern.

CHAPTER TWENTY-FIVE

Comprehending Human Organizational Structure

"RESUME"

NAME: QUINIUS DUPLIUS

- ESTEAMED NOBLE OF HOUSE DUPLIUS, I, QUINIUS DUPLIUS, HAVE BEEN SERVING THE REALM AND THE SHOSTRAN KINGDOM FOR **DECADES!!!** *(that sounds like a lot, right? Should I give the exact number?)*
- THE ABILITIES REQUIRED IN MAINTAINING MY OWN ESTATE QUALIFY ME GRATELY FOR THE OPEN POSITION OF LORD OF THE KINGDOM.

I WISH TO SHOW-CASE THAT FURTHER WITH MY "EXPERIENCES" BELOW

Patriarch of House Duplius
- *1027–1054*

As patriarch of House Duplius, I served to embigger the wealth and prestige of our house while organizing its sub-houses and members into an effective force for positive change. Under me, the house more than **DOUBLED** *in wealth and* **THREED** *in the number of mem-bers. (I want to say I increased the number of members in the house by three times, what's the word for that?)*

Fourman of Duplius Mines
•   1023–1027

As foreman, I was in charge of organizing the miners of our house mines and **KEEPING THEM WORK-ING AT MAXIMUM EFFICIENCY.** *I increased the mine's output by a factor of* **TWO***(!?!) during my*
t   e   n   u   r   e   .

Skillz:
- *Loyalty*
- *Fynance*
- *Mathematics*
- *Culture*
- *Literater*
- *History*

—Poorly written application submitted by Lord Quinius Duplius, who was later forced to abdicate his position to his nephew due to lack of contribution to the war effort

Click found the intruder they were staring at ugly. Tall, powerful, and authoritative were all traits the spider looked up to, but when they were possessed by a bipedal organism covered in soft skin? That wasn't what the [Spider Army Commander] wanted for themself. They'd stick with their eight legs, thorax, and abdomen, thank you very much.

But the intruders' intelligence, combat prowess, and organizational structure were all things Click wanted to bring to the tribe. Or what remained of it, at least.

A small smattering of highly ranked spiders stood around, eager to find some meager entertainment. Too bad the only thing they were capable of finding entertaining was violence. But thankfully, that was enough of a pretense to get them to come along and find something fun *for Click*. In this case, that was trying to better understand how these intruders worked together.

The group of spiders skittered across the cave walls, past the vigilant gazes of the adventurer trio set to guard the dungeon's entrance and made their way to the second floor. The spike trap that had once lain in wait was already deployed, and the sharp spears were cut down into blunt nubs in case it managed to reset itself. But even if worse came to worst, the gaps between the spikes were too wide to harm anyone except the [Bruiser Spider].

Soon enough, Click and their posse found themselves on the second floor's walls and made their way down a long corridor until they came upon a battle in an open room.

"All right, Bolk! You're doing good!" shouted one of the adventurers to a man dressed in heavy armor and holding a shield.

"Is that what it looks like from there, Jaice? Easy? This is anything but—*oof*—easy!" the man shouted back. A Juvenile Dungeon Hound charged into his shield, causing him to take a step back.

"Esmeralda, do something to make Bolk's life easier! Crowd control?" said the first adventurer, Jaice, turning around to address another of their members, a woman in indigo robes.

"Too many of them for that. I'll just make Bolk stronger!" the woman said, raising her arms and letting her flowing sleeves billow as a burst of blue light left her fingertips.

The light struck the one with the shield, Bolk, and his muscles began to roil underneath his skin.

Another Juvenile Dungeon Hound came running at him, and this time he shoved his shield into its face to send it flying back. It took several moments before it recovered and turned back to face him.

"This feels good!" exclaimed Bolk. "But why are we even fighting dungeon hounds? Aren't they supposed to be from the first floor?"

"Maybe they ran down here after we took their old home?" suggested Esmeralda.

"No time to feel bad. They'll be killing villagers if we don't clean this place up first," interjected Jaice. "But enough talking. I'm going to finish them off!"

The man ran in a semi-circle around the predators until his line of sight was perpendicular to Bolk's. Without any fear of hitting his companion, he nocked his shortbow and began to launch arrows at the Juvenile Dungeon Hounds.

The four enemies fell to their attacks, two to arrows and one each to a sword strike by Bolk and a gout of flame by Esmeralda. The three adventurers cheered at their victory and exited the corridor with smiles.

Click watched them the entire time from a safe vantage point with a look of pointed interest. The other spiders had similar looks too, but they were more akin to anticipation, likely feeling hopeful that they'd get to participate in the fight as well.

The [Spider Army Commander] climbed down from the wall and inspected the damage while trying to put the combatants' positions and orders into perspective.

That one intruder, the one the others referred to as Jaice, had a certain directness to their words compared to the others. Combined with their mannerisms, that likely made those words commands. And that likely makes them the one in charge of the other two.

> Skill level up! Decipher Language (6)

The [Spider Bruiser] walked over and began to angrily poke at one of the Juvenile Dungeon Hounds. The large spider was just a bit shorter than the young predator and didn't seem to be too happy about that.

Speaking of short, this particular leader isn't the main *leader of the intruders and is still beholden to the short one. But even in their sub-position, they're able to act by themself to direct their own subordinates into winning a fight.*

Click looked back at the other spiders and let out the equivalent of a sigh.

If only some of my subordinates could also give orders. I'd love to not babysit every fight they get into.

Wham!

A sudden force hit Click on the side and sent the spider flying into a nearby rock.

7 Damage taken! Health: 21/28

What was that?! Click screamed internally as they looked to see what had hit them. A large furry paw was being raised by a small predator on the other end. Small, yet its padded paw was still large enough to send the [Spider Army Commander] sailing.

Where did it come from? Was it also hiding like us? I should've searched the room first! Too late now, though. I'll just have to take care of it! [Command Subor—

Before Click could finish invoking the Skill, the other spiders had already jumped into action.

One of the [Adult Dungeon Spiders] was running around to each of the other spiders and making charade movements with its legs while pointing at the predator. Everyone it communicated with seemed to understand something from the almost erratic movements and jumped into action soon after.

[Bruiser Spider], run up at the enemy.

The large [Bruiser Spider] immediately abandoned the corpse it was inspecting and charged at the still-living predator. It collided with a muted thud as the Juvenile Dungeon Hound went toppling to the ground from the force of the impact.

[Shadow Spiders], run from behind. Bite.

The smaller arachnids did just that, sinking envenomed fangs into the creature's back legs. It let out a yowl but was still too focused on the spider in front of it to act.

[Web Slingers], shoot webs and venom into its eyes.

The red and blue spiders followed their orders, taking semi-calculated potshots that mostly hit fur rather than anything sensitive, but still kept the enemy's focus split.

Click simply stared, watching as the fight progressed. They hadn't invoked [Command Subordinates] even once, yet somehow, they could easily understand what the [Adult Dungeon Spider] was trying to get across.

The Juvenile Dungeon Hound lost balance in its hind paws and began to fall, only to be assisted to the ground by the [Bruiser Spider], who slammed into it while activating [Become Stone]. The large spider's legs acted as a cage to keep the predator's front paws pinned as the others came over and finished it off with additional bites to the jugular. The Juvenile Dungeon Hound's muscles became loose as life left it. The spiders stood up, victorious.

Click walked over and stood up too, not in victory, but in pride.

Maybe I was wrong about you all? they thought.

The spider that directed the attack walked over to its leader and made a bowing motion. It looked familiar to Click, and they realized that it was the same spider that had saved them from the predators when Click had been standing over the [Alpha Hunter]'s corpse way back when.

If anyone's qualified to carry out my orders, it would have to be you. Click nodded back in acceptance of their bow.

Class level up! Anthropologist (4)
Class Skill obtained! Establish Hierarchy

Hey, this looks relevant! I wonder what it does—

Before Click could pull up the System menu, the [Adult Dungeon Spider] before them began to transform, its limbs elongating as its torso lengthened and gained much more mass. The spider before Click was now larger than any other, even rivaling the [Bruiser Spider] by a hair's width.

Even better! What are you now? I haven't seen this evolution before. [Observation]! . . .Oh no.

> Alpha Adult Dungeon Spider (Level 1)
> Soul Link | Rockfort Hamlet Dungeon Core [????????]
> Classes | N/A

[Command Subordinates]! Get over here and kill this a—

The massive spider slowly kneeled before Click.

The [Spider Army Commander], ever vigilant, still completed the command and had the others run towards them. Fangs were bared and ready to kill their fellow spider on their leader's orders. Click waited until the last possible second to call off the attack.

The other spiders stopped just before their limbs could make contact, and Click had them take a step back. A short step.

Click slowly regarded the brand-new alpha before them and, after taking a few more seconds to digest the System table, slowly nodded in acceptance of the newly evolved spider.

It rose, and Click felt . . . happy? There was still fear, but it was superseded by a stronger relief that Click somehow knew to trust.

And then, Click saw it. In that table, under the Soul Link cell, there was a name written next to the gibberish that was normally at the end. It was small, almost totally imperceptible, but it was there. "Click." The [Spider Army Commander]'s name was written right there.

It looks like I have my first sub-leader. You'll be the one to lead the others into battle.

The Alpha Adult Dungeon Spider looked like it couldn't be happier.

CHAPTER TWENTY-SIX

Reclaiming Their Home

Poke.

Click stared intently at the intruders gathering below.

Poke. Poke.

They were discussing something amongst themselves, and Click just *knew* that it was important and didn't want to miss a single word of it.

Poke. Poke. Poke.

What?! the [Spider Army Commander] screamed at the [Adult Alpha] through their command Skill.

The massive spider simply jittered its mandibles while moving its front two legs wildly around.

The action had no explicit meaning, yet the lead spider could simply tell that it meant to convey boredom. Click couldn't really blame the newly evolved spider for feeling that way, since, like all of the other spiders, it was stuck in the web with nothing to do. But unlike those spiders, the [Adult Alpha] decided it was perfectly fine to annoy Click about it.

Poke.

It wanted to go on a hunt, but in the past hour the intruders had all begun to gather around just below the spiders' new web as if waiting for something. Any kind of action on the arachnids' part could alert them and cause their home to be burned down. Again.

Click wasn't going to let it happen. *Again.*

Well, at least it actually listens to me instead of trying to kill me and the rest of the tribe like the old alpha did. That idiot would've grabbed every single spider, pacifist web weavers included, and made them charge straight to their deaths. We wouldn't have even gotten any eggs that way to make a new generation! So, that's one thing to be thankful for.

Poke. Poke.

Argh, fine! How about if I try this new Skill to get you to stop? [Establish Hierarchy]!

Nothing seemed to happen.

Poke. Poke. Poke.

Click felt their legs coil up beneath them in frustration. *What's this Skill even supposed to do?*

Establish Hierarchy
Establish a chain of command among subordinates.

When Click had first obtained it, through some very odd circumstances, they had expected the world from it. But, as it turned out, the Skill didn't really seem to do much. It could've been that Click's tribe wasn't big enough for it to work, or maybe it *did* work, but the effects simply weren't observable yet. But the [Spider Army Commander] felt it would've been nice if it had at least come with a proper description.

Before Click could think of ways to better experiment with the Skill, a heavy set of footsteps echoed from the far passageway, signaling a familiar yet very powerful foe: the leader of the adventurers. A bipedal creature, much shorter than the others—yet somehow towering over them in posture—strutted to the center of the crowd. He let his hammer fall to the ground, and the resulting loud boom got everyone's attention.

"Good news, lads and lasses!" exclaimed the dwarf. His voice echoed off the walls of the cavern and boomed in everyone's ears, though Click was certain he didn't need any special acoustics to do that. "We've done enough damage to the dungeon that it should go inactive after tonight!"

The crowd burst into cheers and continued to make noise for nearly a minute afterwards. Eventually, they calmed down and one of them asked a question.

"Hold on. What about the boss at the end? Who killed it?"

"Nobody did," their leader said, shrugging. "Don't always have to kill the boss to get a dungeon to close up. Works both ways too. Killing it wouldn't have guaranteed a close either."

Click listened in raptly, and even the [Adult Alpha] realized the gravity of the words below and left their own leader alone. [Decipher Language] had gotten fairly high over the last day, and even though it hadn't gotten to level ten—when it would receive a new perk—it was still more than enough to get the general idea of things down below.

The intruders "defeated" the cavern, but failed to defeat the leader? How does this place have a leader? I'm not beholden to anyone! The [Spider Army Commander] felt offended at the idea that they were under the command of a leader who never did anything for them. *Click* was the one keeping the spider tribe alive! But Click soon dismissed the idea as a mistranslation, and continued listening in.

"So, this is it. We're leaving right now and shouldn't have to set foot here until the next cycle!" the dwarf exclaimed.

Another round of cheers went up as people began to walk towards the exit, but a few stood still and tried asking each other questions.

"Hold on. I lost my sword down there!" said one adventurer. "It's a mithril alloy; it's worth a small fortune for my level!"

"And I dropped a few of my potions when one of those dungeon boars cut my potion bag loose! Those cost time and money to make!"

"The loot was surprisingly good, though," interjected a third voice. "Don't tell me that it won't more than make up for it."

"I mean, yeah, but . . . ," began the first adventurer, "it was my first sword. It's got some sentimental value to it, you know."

"Mithril for your first? Talk about spoiled!" said the second adventurer, laughing while patting the first on the back.

"First sword? I can appreciate that, lad," said the dwarf, his boisterous expression now reduced to a personable smolder. "But I can't get these brave men and women to run back down there through deadly traps and monsters just for your sword."

The adventurer began to frown.

"How about this? You tell me about how you got that sword and everything you went through with it over drinks. My treat."

That got them to brighten up.

"There we go! Now, let's leave this dungeon. I heard they're opening up some really old kegs of ale just for us!"

The intruders continued to make their way towards the exit and out the door in single file. Despite how many there were, it didn't take long for them all to leave and for the door to creak shut.

Raid status: Failure! +0 Experience

Click ignored the notification and thought more about the words. Apparently, this was it for the intruders. It sounded like they were finished here and were leaving for good, just like that. The very idea felt bittersweet to Click, who had gotten used to their steady, albeit dangerous, presence these past two days. But most of that feeling came from the loss of their primary study material for their [Anthropologist] Class. Yup, that was definitely it.

But one more thing stood out to the spider. A few of the intruders had dropped their items: so-called "potions," which were what they called those glass vials that held liquids with all sorts of properties, and a sword, one of those large dull-gray weapons they wielded. Actual treasures that could very well make Click, and the rest of the tribe, incomprehensibly stronger.

Click looked back at the few remaining spiders and then at the sac of eggs. With monsters deeper down in the cavern, along with the fact that they apparently got even more powerful the deeper you went, the tribe would need to grow in size and strength to be able to stand a chance down there. And now that the intruders had left, Click could focus all of their efforts on getting everyone into shape.

Poke.

Fine! Let's go on a hunting trip!

The other spiders straightened up and raised their mandibles in a series of smiles.

Click had measured how long had passed between the first and second instances of the intruders entering the dungeon. After they left for what they said was the final time, the spider waited twice the calculated length. Once the final hour of the countdown had passed, Click felt confident that the cavern was now truly theirs again.

Well, it had never actually been theirs, what with the predators roaming around, and after the intruders had passed through, their species was nearly extinct save for a few baby and juvenile variants. And those were no match for the resident alpha.

But before Click could go around asserting their newfound dominance, there was one more important bit of business to take care of.

[Command Subordinates]! Web spiders, weave a web underneath the egg sac with endpoints that extend around the sides of the sac and tie it together at the top. Then, weave a very thick thread that extends for several feet and connect it to the top where it's tied.

The spiders got to work forming a basket around the eggs with a web rope attached.

The first step to rebuilding the tribe was to make sure the eggs hatched in a safe place. And despite how reclusive their location was right now, a ceiling was *not* safe; the baby spiders would simply fall and go *splat* as soon as they hatched. Just like most of the spiders that had gotten hit by the fireball. The ones not immolated had gone flying and, more often than not, landed with a *splat*.

But not the babies. Not them, Click thought to themself while they watched the remaining spiders work on threading the web rope through a curved stalactite and hand it over to several burly spiders. They held onto the rope tightly while the web weavers cut away the webbing below the basket.

The remaining spiders on the web slowly lowered the sac bit by bit, using the curved stalactite as a pulley, until it was on top of the lone spider on the cavern floor.

The [Adult Alpha] was pushed down by the weight of its brethren-to-be but quickly gathered its strength and stood tall. Several Baby and Juvenile Dungeon Hounds were gathered around, watching the scene, but the sheer size and display of strength by the massive spider scared them away. They knew that going for the eggs while the [Adult Alpha] was carrying them would end in the same way as attacking it while it wasn't carrying anything.

The other spiders slowly made their way down from their own mega-web on the ceiling and joined the [Adult Alpha] as it carried the eggs to a relatively remote corner of the cave, away from prying eyes and jaws. It set the sac down and Click breathed the spider equivalent of a sigh of relief.

As the sac touched the ground, the bodies of the eggs' parents fell out. The [Spider Army Commander] slowly walked over and gave them a melancholic stare. *I wanted you all to just stay put, but you laid these eggs instead. You're all idiots. But you're the reason I have any hope for the future. I'm . . . grateful.*

The other spiders stood solemnly for a moment.

Poke.

Click turned to glare at the [Adult Alpha]. *You're* already *bored? It's been five seconds! If that's how you always feel, then I'm going to start calling you that. You're Bored now.*

A quick use of [Command Subordinates] got the information across, and the large spider looked like it agreed with that sentiment. The name stuck.

Sorry, Bored, but we can't go hunting until these eggs are truly *safe. Or at least defensible enough that we don't need every single spider around to guard them. Help us get that done and I'll send you on a hunting trip, okay?*

The [Adult Alpha] spider nodded back.

All right, everyone! [Command Subordinates]! Let's weave a web around these eggs that we'll be proud to call home!

Dear Sir Brimir Steelbeard,

On behalf of the entire hamlet of Rockfort, we thank

you for the service you have done us in defeating the dungeon. The thought that a monster might sneak out and harm us caused great fear in all of us townsfolk, especially the children. The deeds of you and your team have brought us much joy.

We would also like to extend a heartfelt thanks for allowing the members of the Rockfort Raiders adventuring party to retrieve the body of our daughter, Eldia, from the dungeon. We have spent over a year mourning her passing and had no way of truly finding closure while her remains lay in that den of monsters. But the brave work of these three adventurers, who risked their lives to get her back, has given us a means of moving on. And for allowing that, we thank you.

The three adventurers are continuing to recover from their poisoning and shall be staying with us until they are fit enough to move again, though they have told us they wish to stay in the hamlet for much longer, saying it would give them an opportunity to catch up with everyone and get some more training in.

If you or the other adventurers would come by again, we and the whole hamlet would be honored to have you as our guests. The mayor even readied the plans for the construction of a tavern just to allow you all a more comfortable night's sleep! Though, the other townsfolk are fiercely debating its construction since we don't get that many visitors otherwise.

So thank you once more for your services, and may the gods watch over you all. They did so for us by having you all come here.

Sincerely,
Pulma and Rolpho
Shepherd, Eldia's parents

About the Author

V. Nator is a giant nerd who does it all: writes novels, makes Minecraft modpacks, and bakes. A lot of people happen to really like the words he writes.